To Whom it May Concern

A family in crisis

HILTON JONES

Cover design by: Peter H Jones

ONE

Chrissy Chisholm awoke slowly, almost afraid to open her eyes. She had experienced room-spin before and was reluctant to find out if the previous night's excesses would produce a repeat performance.

After all, it had been her hen-night. If she couldn't get drunk on her hen night, when could she?

Slowly, she replayed the evening's events, from arriving at the Cumberland Arms with Linda and Aanya, her long-term friends since primary school days. Three trainee nurses together, they knew all about each other. They told each other everything. There were no secrets. Family news, nurses' home gossip, boyfriend secrets, nothing was off limits, yet.

The Cumberland Arms had been a good choice of venue. Close enough to the nurses' home for them to walk home afterwards and smart enough to enable the girls to enjoy dressing up for a posh night out.

The Cumberland was approached by a flight of stone steps, almost the width of the façade, with judicially placed handrails at intervals for those who needed assistance to mount the fifteen steps to the revolving doors at the entrance. Once inside, guests found a deeply-carpeted foyer leading to a curved brass-rimmed reception desk, its marble surface reflecting the myriad down lighters sparkling like so many stars in the navy-blue ceiling. Behind the desk, a smiling, uniformed receptionist greeted guests and directed them to their rooms, having ensured a porter was on hand to carry their luggage. Non-residents were directed to the various meeting rooms or the lounge bar, restaurant, spa or ballroom as required. The restaurant had a reputation for good food, having attracted a celebrity chef to join the staff. Hence the choice of the Cumberland Arms for her hen-night.

It was certainly a better choice for the girls than David's for his stag night. The Ram's Head Inn sat under a thatched roof, its ancient appearance outside matched by the rustic style of the interior. Timbered walls supported heavy hand-hewn beams which endangered the heads of anyone over six feet tall. A smoke-blackened fireplace which, in winter, blazed with a well-tended log fire added to the comfortable atmosphere, its flames reflecting off the polished brass ornaments which adorned every shelf, nook and cranny around the walls.

BMW's and Mercs in the Cumberland car park; Ford pick-ups and souped-up Mini's at the Ram's Head; that gave an indication of what to expect inside. Both places were popular with their particular clientele and were full on most nights of the week. Last night had been no exception.

Chrissy looked back over the evening. They had all arrived on time, twenty young women intent on enjoying themselves, roughly half from the nurses' home, the rest made up of Chrissy's friends from outside the profession, school friends, neighbours and other acquaintances. Greeted with cocktails, they sat down in the sumptuous dining room to a meal from the Cumberland's extensive menu. It was an almost formal start to the proceedings, but as the wine flowed, so did the conversation and the two groups soon broke down whatever barriers which might have stood between them. Informality reigned and they became a noisy, happy band of sisters, hell-bent on enjoying themselves come what may. Following the meal they adjourned to the bar where tales, drawing heavily on their past experiences, (Do you remember when..?) bounced back and forth, punctuated by screams and peals of laughter which echoed through the whole of the Cumberland Arms.

Linda and Aanya had a self-imposed task of looking after Chrissy without their charge's knowledge and they had kept a close eye on what she drank but as the evening wore on, their vigilance relaxed. The arrival of Tom Collins and Bloody Mary put paid to any of their serious plans of caring for the bride-to-be.

Chrissy pieced this jigsaw of events together as her mind became clearer. She smiled inwardly as she replayed in her mind the raucous chorus of 'Here comes the Bride', though she had trouble recalling the remainder of what was likely to be a bawdy lyric. It was probably better not to remember some things, though what the management, staff and other hotel guests would have made of it didn't bear thinking about.

She tried mentally listing her drinks; she only had a few so it should be simple, or so she thought. As she got further through the list it became obvious why she was having trouble recalling most of what happened. An almost suicidal combination of wines and spirits, cocktails and liqueurs had passed over her lips and she found it difficult to recall the latter part of the evening's jollifications. Had it been jolly? Her right knee was sore, but at this point she could not summon the courage to bend over in the bed to look at it. Had she fallen over? She didn't remember falling.

She remembered that some of the boys from David's stag party had turned up later, just as the girls were leaving. Brett was meeting Charlotte. Lucky devils. Flying out to Australia today to a career in a Sydney hospital.

She remembered the two groups milling about on the pavement outside the Cumberland, the boys making as much noise as the girls. A memory of good night kisses as the girls dispersed. A fleeting glimpse of David as he was whisked away to his taxi with only a peck on the cheek. Walking to the nurses' home. A broken heel on her shoe as she stepped off the kerb. Is that why her knee is sore? So she did fall. Gary supported her as she limped in a drunken haze. Did he help her up the staircase? Why was she feeling doubtful about Gary? She would never have managed that interminable flight of stairs alone. 'Stairway to Heaven' Gary called it. The intensity of the memories grew less as she went on, unable to recall details. It was just as well she was here, in bed, trying to sleep it off.

She sat up suddenly, ignoring the headache and the attempts of her brain to stop itself swirling about in her skull. 'I'm naked. Who undressed me? Was it Gary? What else did he do? Did he…..?'

She sank back into the pillows, tortured by her thoughts. She couldn't ask anyone what had happened. Partly because she was afraid of the answer, partly because she didn't know who to ask. Not Gary for sure. 'Did we have sex last night?' would get either a yes from him, which she didn't want to hear, or a no, which would probably be a lie so she would still be no wiser. Gary was not the type who would keep it to himself and David would find out two days before the wedding. She couldn't ask Linda or Aanya. They had gone ahead; she had a vague memory of them leaving and saying goodbyes to the last of the revellers, so they wouldn't know.

She would go to the altar on Saturday with a big

secret in her mind.

The stag night at the Ram's Head had gone very well, as stag nights go. David and Chrissy had decided not to go along with the current fashion of a boat trip to Ireland or a flight to Latvia for their celebrations. Instead, they settled for a more traditional celebration in familiar surroundings on home ground, which would ensure that all their friends would be able to join them without worrying about the cost. So David and his fellow young doctors, all newly qualified, enjoyed an uproarious time at the Ram's Head. Just as the girls had done, they related events from their past interspersed with jokes which got more puerile and generated evermore raucous laughter as the evening progressed. Drinking games were played, the best of which involved a glass boot which held two pints of beer. This was filled and passed around to see who could drink it all without spilling a drop. If a drinker spilt any, he paid to top it up and the boot was passed on to the next contestant. Many a drinker thought he was doing well until, if the toe of the boot pointed upwards, a sudden rush of air into the toe as the beer level went down pushed a tsunami of beer out of the boot and down the shirt front of the unfortunate drinker, to the loud amusement of the rest of the party.

Only Gary managed to complete the task successfully, having worked out that it was necessary to keep the toe of the boot pointing out to the side, preventing a vacuum developing in the toe as the beer level went down.

The evening was helped by the large platter of chips, barbequed sausages and chicken wings provided by the management, whose generosity was immediately recompensed by a rush to the bar.

David was living outside the town with his father and had sensibly ordered a taxi rather than take the risk of driving home, so when the party broke up and they spilled out noisily on to the pavement, he went along with the throng towards the car park in the hope of seeing Chrissy and ensuring that she was alright to walk home. As they passed the Cumberland Arms, they met the girls disgorging from Chrissy's hen party. Chaos ensued as they all cheered, shouted, laughed and screeched their goodnights to each other.

David managed to find Chrissy in the melee, but could only manage a peck on the cheek before she was whisked away by one of her friends and he had to return to the Ram's Head to meet his taxi.

As the crowd thinned out, Chrissy found herself almost alone and made her way, stumbling towards the nurses' home. Gary walked beside her and, as she tripped off the kerb, she went down on one knee. Gary was quick to help her to her feet, and almost too quick to check her injured knee, his hand sliding uncomfortably above her knee momentarily during his examination. He diagnosed a slight graze with a smear of blood which he wiped away with his handkerchief, then discovered that the heel of her shoe had broken off in the fall.

They made their way to the nurses' home. This was housed in a tall Victorian building which had started life as a workhouse, a home for the poor and needy. 150 years previously. Victorian philanthropists felt the need to announce their good deeds to all and sundry by building imposing edifices, usually on high ground, to impress on the poor how much they owed to their benefactors. Consequently, when the modern St Agnes' Hospital had been built in the grounds in later years, a long staircase had been added to provide access to the rear of the building as the workhouse was adapted to provide accommodation, initially dormitory, but now individual rooms, for the nurses.

With Gary's arm around her waist, Chrissy made her way to the foot of the staircase, took one despairing look at the climb ahead and passed out.

TWO

'Isn't it great? Gary's agreed to give me some driving lessons in his car. So you won't have the expense of a driving school.'

'Yes, Jonathan. It sounds good.'

Dr David Maitland was always one to take a measured view of things and the use of his son's full name gave the boy a hint that the comment to follow would not be favourable. Rushing into an arrangement for Jonathan to have driving lessons with Gary was not David's style. Although he had known Gary since their Med School days there had always been a sense of untrustworthiness about him. He was a good doctor, neither brilliant nor ambitious, and had not followed the same path of improvement and promotion that had marked David's progress through his career, which culminated in his post as cardiologist at St Agnes' Hospital.

While Gary had remained at Aggies for most of the intervening years, David had enjoyed placements all over the country, a GP practice in Cornwall, ten weeks at a hospital in Nottingham, even a three-month stint in the Barbados Blood Transfusion Service, gaining varied experience in different specialties. His foundation years in Newcastle included general surgery and cardiology, which seemed to offer the best of both worlds with a combination of medicine and practical procedures. He therefore came back to Aggies as a respected cardiologist, having chosen this hospital to be near his ailing father at his home in Cheshire.

David had maintained contact with Gary on his

frequent visits to his father, mainly because others of their med school colleagues were scattered far and wide – Brett was still in Australia, Colin and James in London, two others had followed the money and gone to the States. They had been friends, therefore, for years and Gary had been 'Uncle Gary' to David's children, Jonathan and Maddy, when they were little, though the unofficial title had been dropped as they grew older.

'That sounds as though it's going to be followed with a 'but',' Jon said.

'Yes, it is,' his father said, 'but there's all the theory to learn as well. Gary has been driving for years. He's an experienced driver, but I don't want you learning all his bad habits alongside everything else. I still think you'll be better off at a driving school. Perhaps a few drives with Gary later will give you some road experience when you've learned the basics'

'Suits me fine. Thanks, Dad'

As Jon started to leave the room, his father added

'And by the way, Jon, don't get any ideas about a new car. We'll get you something sensible, and second hand, once you've passed your test.'

'Yes, Dad' was spoken in a way only teenagers can manage for sullen acceptance of parental decisions, his dreams of something racy dashed in a sentence.

'Get yourself a copy of the Highway Code when you're in town,' his mother threw in. 'You can't start too early learning the rules. I can ask you some questions from it.'

'Good idea, Mum' was spoken in a much more upbeat way.

As the door closed behind Jon, Chrissy smiled across at David.

'He needs a bit of encouragement as well, you know, though I agree that too much training with Gary might be overdoing it.'

'You've never trusted Gary, have you?' David said. 'Any reason?'

Chrissy looked down, avoiding his gaze, hoping she looked casual. She couldn't mention the doubt she had carried all their married life. Eighteen years of wondering, watching for similarities. Hair colour, eyes, mannerisms. Was there anything of Gary in Jon? What had really happened after the hen party?

'Well, he's not exactly sleazy, but there always seems to be something else, something shady, going on in his life. Gambling runs away with his money. He's got a lovely partner but I don't know how Sheryl puts up with him, the way he looks at the student nurses, for instance. His smutty jokes with the patients. Someone is going to complain, one day. Yet he's always been nice to our two, especially Jon.'

She shuddered slightly, hoping David hadn't noticed, as the thought of Gary as Jon's father crossed her mind once more.

* * * *

Vince Spivey was enjoying himself. Deliveries close to home in the streets of Liverpool were done by his taxi drivers and sometimes children, who he managed to coerce into working for him, but he always kept the Welsh deliveries to himself. This gave him the chance to open out his Goldwing along the A55 on the return journey to Liverpool. On the outward journey he was a model driver, as he didn't want to attract the attention of the North Wales Police cars, which waited to apprehend speed merchants on the Expressway. So speed limits

10

were observed, especially that 50mph area around Colwyn Bay, which could catch you out if you were not aware of its existence. His overtaking was never reckless; signals were clear and timely; there wasn't a more courteous driver on the road. But with his drugs delivered and five thousand pounds, sometimes double that, hidden in the false bottom of his panniers, he gave full rein to the power of his bike for much of the way home.

* * * *

'Why do we have to go home?' Celia asked.

'Because we live there' her brother replied. At two years her senior, he thought he was qualified to answer.

'Shut up, Carl. You don't know everything. You're only seven,' Celia responded.

'And you're five and you don't know anything!'

'Will you two just settle down,' Jess, their mother, said from the front seat of their Ford Focus, as they made their way home from a fraught weekend at the seaside. 'You've ruined our little holiday with your arguing.'

'It's his fault,' Celia said. 'He broke my spade, so I couldn't build a proper sandcastle. I hate him!'

Their father, Michael, finally came to the end of his patience. 'Look, you two. I'm trying to concentrate on driving in this traffic so do as your mother says and settle down. Find something quiet to play with.'

Carl picked up their kite, which had flown moderately well all weekend, out of the foot-well.

'I'll play with the kite,'

'I want it, Carl'

'Get off. Don't pull it.'

'It's mine.'

At a tearing sound from the back seat, Michael turned his head,

'If you've torn that…'

A scream from Jess brought Michael's attention back to the road ahead as the preceding car pulled out to overtake a slow-moving caravan, leaving a rapidly closing gap of which Michael, his attention on the turmoil in the back seat, was completely unaware. He turned the wheel quickly to his right to avoid the caravan and only noticed at the last minute the bright headlight of a following motorcycle which had appeared as if from nowhere in his rear-view mirror. It swung to the right, narrowly missing their car, then, as the motorcyclist over-corrected in trying to avoid the Armco barrier, it swung sideways across the motorway in front of them. Vince struggled to keep his steed upright and travelled along the hard shoulder for some yards, braking hard. He saw the Focus continuing and as he slowed, the caravan overtook him.

'Bloody idiots!' he yelled, to no-one in particular, or the world in general.

Still doing thirty, he ran into a discarded lorry tyre and was thrown sideways from his now stationary bike. Stiff blackthorns pierced his leathers, and as he yelled his discomfort, lying in the bushes, he saw his Goldwing overbalancing towards him.

'No… no…'he screamed.

He knew his bike weighed over a ton, as he struggled, unsuccessfully, to escape the grip of the thorns. There was a loud crack and he was fortunate that the combination of the thickness of the undergrowth and the angle of the handlebars created a bridge over his upper body. He was unfortunate that the loud crack came from his shin bone as it was broken cleanly by the

they had long conversations over his final drink as she washed glasses and put the chairs on the tables to give the morning's cleaners clear access to the floor. In that period, they went through the sequence of being friends, then good friends, lovers and partners. Sheryl was quite aware that she didn't know everything there was to know about Gary, so she had not taken the final step in the sequence to become his wife but was quite happy to remain as partner, if only for the welfare of their son, Duncan, who had inherited his father's good looks.

Gary was also an inveterate gambler. Horse, dogs, sport (football, rugby, snooker, boxing it didn't matter what), Gary was always ready to place a bet, and like so many gamblers, he lost more than he won and Sheryl had a mountainous struggle to keep the housekeeping in order. Fortunately, his doctor's salary kept them afloat, but only just.

It was later that day that Gary returned to Vince's bedside.

'Well, Mr Spivey, it seems that bush did you a real favour. It cushioned your fall and ensured that your bike didn't crush you against a hard surface. If you had been on the tarmac, for instance, your injuries would have been much more serious. As it is, you have some bruising on your hip and your chest, but nothing is wrong internally.'

'Great. So I can go home, then?'

'Yes. I'll give you a prescription for a bit of pain relief which will keep you comfortable for a few days. Ibuprofen will keep you pain-free after that.'

'What if I have terrible pain? Could you give me something stronger?'

'Well, yes. But you shouldn't need it.'

'Morphine, for instance?'

'That would be far too strong.'

'But if I felt I needed it, I might be reconsidering my decision about reporting....' He left the sentence hanging as Gary's expression told him that the penny was dropping.

'You wouldn't'

The words were a cross between a statement and a question. Gary had never faced this problem before. His mind raced. Had he really insulted the nurse? Was she likely to confirm Vince's accusation? What would the Board's attitude be? Would it come to a tribunal? Could he be suspended...surely not struck off? But supplying drugs to a patient? That was another matter entirely. He couldn't prescribe morphine for a broken leg, especially if there were no complications. This was just a simple transverse fracture. The auditors would spot it a mile off. He would have to steal it, falsify the records. And that would leave him open to all sorts of problems.

'You don't know how I'd feel if the pain got too bad.' Vince knew he had the upper hand.

'I'll have to think about it,' Gary said and started gathering his papers.

'Well don't think for too long. I'm still leaving this afternoon, aren't I?'

'Yes, of course.' Gary said and left. Vince smiled a self-satisfied smile at Gary's departing back.

In Ward 7, Billy Welford was gasping for air. Dr David Maitland had drawn the curtains around his bed while he examined the unfortunate Billy. His angina had progressed to something more serious and he was in danger of a heart attack. The pains in his chest were excruciating and he had difficulty getting even a word out to explain how he felt. He struggled to pull at the tubes that were attached to his body in an effort to pull himself upright, not realising they were keeping him alive, and eventually dragged his drip feed over, crashing to the floor. David called for help as he pacified his patient. Fortunately, a nurse was at hand with her drugs trolley and she rushed in, picking up the drip and reconnecting it. 'GTN quickly,' David said and she administered a dose of glyceral trinitrate under Billy's tongue to calm him down.

Her unattended trolley stood just inside the door as Gary passed down the corridor, desperately thinking of how to satisfy Vince's demands. The crash in Ward 7 caused him to look in as he passed. The open lid of the drugs trolley was an invitation. He didn't even pause to thank the gods. He reached in and helped himself to a jar of tablets which he knew, without checking the label, were Morphine. The attention of the occupants of Ward 7, patients and staff, was on Billy and his problem. The only bit of excitement they had had today. Gary continued down the crowded corridor with more of a spring in his step.

Later that afternoon, Vince was ready to leave. His mate, Terry, pulled up at the main door in Vince's BMW and Vince hobbled out on unfamiliar crutches, helped by Gary, who took the opportunity to surreptitiously slip a small jar of tablets into Vince's coat pocket.

'I'll be in touch,' Vince said, and a cold chill ran up Gary's back as he realised that he'd been hooked. This was not the end; it was the beginning. A sprat to catch a mackerel. He knew he'd never be free of the threat of blackmail – on a slippery road to who knows where.

On his way home he called in to see Barry Meadows

at his betting shop. Against the tinny background of race readers' commentary, and with not a little trepidation, he asked Vera if Barry was in and could he see him for a minute, please? He never knew how Vera would react. Top end of middle age, with iron-grey hair tightly pulled back into a pony tail which extended quite a way down her back, she had the temperament of a rottweiler – sometimes docile and sometimes something to be avoided at all costs. He had seen her in that mood with punters who tried to bring in cans of lager as they tried to win that fortune that was dangling temptingly in the next race and they must get the bet on before the off. Gary also knew her soft side, as gentle as the angel that she really was with her disabled son when she brought him into the hospital following accidents to which he was prone. Her stern disposition was reserved for the betting shop and the fact that she knew Gary from the hospital tempered her reaction to him only a little on the occasions when he asked to see her boss. It was inevitably the pre-amble to a request for time to pay. She nodded and vanished through the office door behind her, to return a minute later, followed by Barry Meadows, a round-faced, round-bellied, red-cheeked man who could have been designed on a seaside postcard.

'What can I do for you today, Gary?' he asked, through the grill which separated the punters from the staff. As he spoke, he picked up the piece of paper which Vera had pushed across the counter.

'I was hoping you'd be able to grant me a little credit until the weekend, Barry. Not a lot. Just fifty quid. I've had a tip and I'm more than pretty sure it will pay off.'

Barry looked at the paper that Vera had passed to him. 'You didn't do so well today, did you? It looks as though you owe me three hundred already and today's winnings were just twenty quid. If you keep borrowing at this rate it'll be a grand by the end of the month.'

'I'll be able to pay it all off by then, pay day and all that. It's just a couple of weeks. You know I'm good for it.'

'But it keeps happening, Gary. I'm not the Bank of England, you know. Have you thought of giving it a rest? Just until you can get yourself straight. I'm sure Sheryl would appreciate it as well.'

'I never thought I'd hear a bookmaker tell a punter to give up betting,' Gary said with a smile.

'Well, I'm not a bookmaker to you, am I? I'm a money lender. Just this once, then. Fifty quid. And you'd better pray that this horse comes in for you. Vera will make sure you pay it off.'

'No need to worry. This is a cert. See you next week,' and he left, hoping that Sheryl wouldn't find out that he was in debt to the bookies once again.

FOUR

'Surprise! Surprise!'

Chrissy's eyes lit up as she opened the door to this most pleasant announcement.

'Linda! Aanya! How wonderful. But what …'

The rest of her greeting was muffled by the hugs and kisses from her friends, so tight as though to make up for all the lost time since they had last met.

They followed her into the house, explaining as they went that they had been accompanying a patient transferred from the Doncaster hospital where they both worked to the paediatric department at Aggies for specialist treatment.

Linda explained, 'It was only this morning that it was decided to make the transfer. The poor little lad needed urgent care on the journey so we volunteered…'

'Linda was always pushy; she calls it volunteering, but it worked this time,' put in Aanya, with a smile.

'Well, when I heard he was coming here it was too good a chance to miss. It's ages since we've seen you, so it was a case of two birds, one stone.'

'I'm so glad you made it happen. You're the tonic I need at the moment,' Chrissy said. 'David's father is very ill – he's not expected to last the week out. Cancer, of course, so we're all very worried.'

Chrissy led the way out of the reception hall through bi-fold doors into a spacious L-shaped kitchen/dining room. There was an extensive range of contemporary high gloss grey wall and floor units with modern integrated appliances. A flight of steps led down to a fitted bar, while the open-plan dining area had a large picture window with views of a well-kept and well-stocked kitchen garden with manicured lawns beyond. The girls took it all in, admiring what they saw as Chrissy put the kettle on – the girls were still at work, so G and T was out of the question.

The new arrivals hadn't long for their visit and the conversation took up almost seamlessly where it had left off the last time they met, just as when they were at school. Their children were all about the same age, at the top end of secondary school. Linda's daughter was looking forward to going to university to study for a degree in Engineering, prior to joining her father's engineering company. Aanya's two boys were into IT and her daughter was setting her sights on Bollywood. Her fine Indian features, inherited from her mother, would surely attract interest from producers, they thought, but as she was only twelve years old there was time yet for her ambitions to change.

'Is this your two?' Linda asked, picking up a framed photograph from the sideboard.

'Yes. Maddy is going into sixth form and Jon's having a year off. He can't make up his mind what to do. At the moment, he's learning to drive. Gary's teaching him.'

'Gary? Not Gary Baker. Not watch-out-for-the-baker-you'll-get-a-bun-in-the-oven Gary Baker? Is he still here?'

The plate Chrissy was carrying crashed as it hit the tiled kitchen floor.

'It's alright. I'll clear it up,' she said, taking a dustpan and brush from the cupboard under the sink to cover her confusion. Her voice shook with emotion and her old friends immediately recognised the signs that all was not well. A look passed between them as they rushed to help.

Linda took the dustpan from her with, 'I'll do that' while Aanya, put an arm around Chrissy's shoulder, guided her towards a sofa in the nearby lounge. Having binned the broken china, Linda joined them and the two sat either side of her.

'What was that all about?' Linda asked, direct as ever.

'N-nothing. It just slipped out of my hands.' Chrissy was twisting her handkerchief in her hands. Her voice was still shaky.

Perceptively, Aanya said, 'Why did the mention of Gary make you drop the plate?'

The tears started, tears of relief. She felt safe with her old friends and perhaps now was the time to tell them of her worries. She dabbed at her eyes as she related what she remembered of the hen night and the doubts which had dogged her waking thoughts ever since. 'I had to tell someone, so I told my mum and she promised never to mention it to anyone. And Gary's never mentioned it since, perhaps one or two of his suggestive remarks now and again could have been hints, but nothing definite, just hints. But then he makes remarks like that to nurses, patients, whoever. But I can't be sure. And that photograph you picked up. Jon has some of Gary's features, doesn't he?'

'They're both good looking men, there's bound to be similarities. You must be imagining it.' Practical Linda took a straightforward line as if to expunge the thoughts that crossed and recrossed Chrissy's mind.

'They're both tall; so is David. They both have brown eyes. So does David, most people do. I'm sure Gary would have given you more indication if he had taken you to bed that night.' Aanya was soothing and reassuring.

'We should never have left here. But we all had new husbands, new jobs.' Aanya said. 'And you didn't say anything, so we didn't know.'

'You could have told us. We'd have got the truth out of Gary somehow.' That was Linda again.

'I was so ashamed. And when I found I was pregnant so soon after the wedding...'

'You could still have told us that night. Shouted to us. Anything.'

'But I was drunk, Linda. Absolutely plastered. You two had gone ahead of me. There's no one else I could ask and Gary has always been so nice to Jon; he's OK with Maddy but it's obvious that Jon's his favourite. There are times when it all gets too much for me and I wish Gary wasn't here any more. I know that sounds awful, but I can't help it.' Chrissy's tears were abating. 'Still, you don't want to listen to my problems. You've got to get back to Doncaster. The kettle's boiling, so let's have a cup of tea before you set off. We can talk about something else.'

The mundane effort of preparing tea and biscuits helped her to regain her composure and they spent a pleasant hour catching up and reminiscing as old friends do. The time to leave arrived all too soon and they parted with hugs and kisses and promises to keep in touch. Chrissy hoped they would.

FIVE

David Maitland was very close to his father. Alistair Maitland had been a doctor in General Practice, popular in his Cheshire village where he had practised for 40 years. Assisted by his late wife, Marjorie, he had ministered to a large farming area with a mixture of caring, good humour and generosity, which were repaid by similar sentiments from the population at large.

After Marjorie had passed away, David had come to live with his father while studying at Aggie's, a nickname, incidentally, which Alistair detested as being disrespectful. 'It makes it sound like a pie shop,' he often said.

David had entered the profession not from any parental pressure, rather as a result of the respect which was shown to Alistair. His father never pushed him; he just made things possible, like suggesting that there would be no better time to get married than at the end of medical school as both he and Chrissy would be free from other commitments.

Marjorie had written a successful book on nursing, which was used as a text book in many teaching hospitals, and the royalties after her death passed to David in her will, so the young couple were able to start married life without the money worries experienced by many other newly-weds.

There was a general feeling of sadness in the whole community when the news went round that Alistair was seriously ill. His popularity in the village was also felt in the hospital, through the many referrals of his patients over the years. He was a regular visitor, too, taking the opportunity to pop into the wards to visit patients if he happened to be there for meetings of the Health Board and the like. As a result, not only was he well-known, he was also well cared-for at Aggies.

'Sorry to hear about your father,' Gary sympathised with David as they met in the corridor of the hospital.

'Thanks, Gary. It's very sad, but... well, you know how it is.' Even with all their medical knowledge and experience, doctors fall into the same platitudes as the rest of us in times of family distress, when the inevitable finality of a diagnosis manifests itself.

'Big C, did someone say?'

'Yes. Terminal.' David replied. 'Nothing we can do,' he added. 'He's only been ill for a few weeks. In a way, that could be a blessing. He won't suffer the pain for long. That's the worst part of it all. The pain. All the palliative treatments in the world won't take the pain away. He has come to terms with the finality of it. He's a doctor, after all, and he's seen hundreds of patients going through the same thing over the years, so he knows exactly what's going on, but it hurts me to see him in such pain all the time'

'Of course. I'm really sorry about it. It's been an honour to know him. What's the prognosis, time-wise?'

'Could be any time, Jim Parton says.'

'Jim's a good oncologist. I'm sure he'll do his best for him. Give your Dad my regards when you see him.'

'Thanks, I will,' David said to Gary's departing back, then hurried off to make what turned out to be his final visit to his father's bedside.

The old man was weak, his breathing gentle. Their eyes met and Alistair lifted one hand off the bed, his attempt at a farewell wave. David detected the beginnings of a smile, then the eyes closed and gradually the breathing stopped, the colour changed from the sickly yellow to alabaster white. Doctor Alistair Maitland was finally at peace.

David sat and held his father's lifeless hand, feeling the temperature change. Tears streamed down his face as he said his goodbyes. 'Thanks for being a great Dad. You gave me everything – ambition, a shining example to follow – I wanted to make you proud of me. I hope I did. I hope I am as good a Dad to the kids as you were to me. I don't know what to……' He took in a deep breath and dried his eyes. '…. Bye, Dad, and God Bless.'

He got up and, with a final backward look at his father, he left the room, leaving the nurse who had responded to the insistent note of the monitor to take over the final procedures.

David's journey home that evening seemed to go on for ever. He didn't look forward to telling Chrissy and the kids the sad news, even though they were expecting it. It would still come as a shock. The 'blessed relief' emotions come later to ease the pain of parting, though the sadness never really goes away.

When he arrived home, he found Chrissy's mother, Alexandra, was also waiting for news. An athletic 73year-old standing at five-foot-four, she had just been telling Jonathan about her latest golf success – the Ladies Cup – which she had won by 10 strokes, 8 under par at The Oaks Golf Club on the outskirts of the village.

'You should take up golf, my lad' she said in her usual hearty manner. 'Do you good, you know. Out in the fresh air. Exercise. Precision. Concentration. And it gives you a change from studying.'

'Well, I've given up studying for a while, Gran. I'm

having a year off.'

'All the more reason to have something to do. Can't have my favourite grandson going to the dogs!'

'I'm your only grandson, Gran.'

'So that's why I'm trying to see to your welfare. Your future is at stake unless you invest your time and brains into it now, while you are young enough to learn. I know exactly how you feel. I was fed up with school and exams so I left when I was 16. I had always liked English lessons, writing stories and so on, so I wrote a report on the village flower and vegetable show and sent it to the Chester Chronicle. It didn't get published, but the editor asked me to come in and have a word. He obviously saw something in me and I never looked back. By the time I was 25, I was on TV, reporting for the BBC from all over the world.'

'Yes, Mum said you were on telly. Our foreign correspondent, Zandra Martin, she said you were. Sounds rather grand, doesn't it?'

'I suppose it does. Yes, that was my maiden name. I went back to using Alex after I left the BBC; it's less conspicuous than Zandra, don't you think?'

Jon nodded; Alex went on.

' I met all sorts of people, from presidents and generals in Africa to astronauts in America and starving mums in Ethiopia.'

'But wasn't it dangerous sometimes?' Jon wanted to know.

'Occasionally, but there was always plenty of security about. You would only see me on the screen but there would be some big fellows in the background to look after me.'

She omitted to mention events which would have

stood Jon's hair on end. Like the occasion when there was no security man with her in her tent and a Nigerian war-lord took advantage of the situation. He came up behind her with obvious plans. 'And now, little lady…' was as far as he got in his foreplay as she spun round. Her right hand went to his testicles and squeezed, hard, occasioning a sharp intake of breath which was immediately stifled by her left hand taking a tight grip on his windpipe. As her manicured nails dug into his flesh, his eyes rolled due to the pain and the shortage of breath, his arms flailed and his legs felt weak. Tears of pain dripped off his chin as he crumpled to the ground. Zandra stood over him and said, 'I am here as a reporter, not for your pleasure. Now get out of my tent.' He left on all fours and wore a red and white neckerchief for some days after that to cover the deep bruising on his neck. None of his men dared to enquire as to why this addition to his wardrobe had suddenly appeared. They surmised that it might be something to do with him crawling out of Zandra's tent the evening before, though the sharp-eyed mercenary who had witnessed this and broke the news to his mates would have denied all knowledge of it had anyone enquired. Zandra, however, had no more trouble from that quarter.

'But you've seen some awful things as well, haven't you?' Jon went on.'

'Oh, yes. Victims of earthquakes and other disasters. Plane crashes. Casualties of shootings. Probably the saddest were starving people in Africa. That's where I met your grandfather. Anthony was working for a charity, Food for Africa. He was a wonderful man.'

'Let me guess. That was why you married him, was it?' Jon put in.'

Alex smiled at the memory.

'Yes,' she said. 'Then I started working for the charity after your mother was born.'

'So you left the BBC when you got married?'

'Soon after. We found that married life and foreign correspondent didn't go together. Then Chrissy was born so I stayed at home. As soon as she went to school, I took a job doing admin for the charity. It was a few years later that they sent your grandfather and me off to Africa to manage their work out there. We came home fairly frequently, for your mum and dad's wedding, for instance, then again a year later when you were born. I had to meet my first grandson, didn't I?'

She ruffled his hair.

'It was worth the long journey to see my little boy!'

'But you didn't come back when Maddy was born.' There was always a bit of sibling rivalry and Jon was quick to score a point over his sister.

'No. I was nursing your grandfather. He'd contracted malaria and was very ill at the time. Sadly, he died shortly afterwards, so a visit to see your new sister had to wait.'

'Oh, I'm sorry' Jon said, as much an apology to Maddy as to his grandmother, and mentally deducted the point he thought he'd scored.

David arrived home with the sad news from his father's bedside, which he imparted to the family all together, having called Chrissy and Maddy in from the kitchen. Tears and sympathetic hugs followed, together with the beginnings of plans for the funeral. They were all lost in their own thoughts, emotions and memories. David's thoughts hopped about the practicalities. Engaging a funeral director. Barton's would be doing it. Well-established family firm. Alistair had insisted on this.

He and Aubrey Barton, the current owner, had overseen the departure of most of the population of the area who had died in the last 40 years. Indeed, they had a long-standing, -perhaps, tongue-in-cheek- arrangement that whichever of them died first, the other was to deal with his final departure. Then there was booking the church and the vicar, David wanted to do the right thing for his father so everything had to be spot-on. A horse-drawn bier would be over the top. There would be hundreds of mourners, both lining the road up to St Winifred's Anglican Church and in the church itself, such was the esteem in which Alistair was held in the county. Barton's would see to the crematorium – another of Alistair's stipulations. The Cumberland Arms would cope with the wake; their function room would be filled to overflowing, he was sure.

Chrissy, on the other hand, was concerned with the family, how they would be dressed for the funeral. For a man with Alistair's reputation there would need to be a degree of formality. So black would need to be in evidence, but Alistair had such a lively, outgoing personality that there should be a plenty of colour as well. Flowers were an obvious choice, both in the hearse and at the church. But what else could she do? As Alistair had been proud of his connection with St Agnes' Hospital, she hit on the idea of ribbons in the colours of the hospital coat of arms, royal blue, yellow and green, instead of black ribbons on the hearse.

Jon and Maddy sat close. Sibling rivalry was abated temporarily, as they comforted each other with proximity. No words would help. This was a new experience for them. There were no memories of previous bereavements to help them through the pain of losing a beloved grandparent. Both David's mother and Chrissy's father had died either before or soon after they were born. The gap left by Alistair in their lives was new territory. No longer could they say 'I must tell Grandpa' when they had news of a success at school or on the sports field. No longer would the aroma of his aftershave linger in their nostrils after he had visited.

Alex was quiet. She had seen death in all its horror all over the world and reported on it, dispassionately, but when it came knocking on your own door, it's quite a different matter. Alistair had become a good friend over the years and she would miss him terribly. Her mind went back to Africa, when Anthony had died. The torment she felt then at his passing had been unbearable, watching him suffer the fevers of malaria and his tortured finality at the end. Her reputation as a little toughie who could cope with anything counted for nothing. She hoped that her grandchildren would never have to experience that feeling of helplessness. Looking at them now, huddled together on the settee, she was not so sure. They had watched Alistair's swift decline as the pain took its toll on his body. She realised that she was more concerned about Jon than Maddy. Perhaps because he was older? She knew you shouldn't have favourites but Maddy seemed stronger, more headstrong, than her brother in many ways, very much the dare-devil. Or did she just seem that way to a grandmother who had missed the birth and early life of her grand-daughter and so had not bonded to the same extent. Jon was definitely her favourite.

SIX

About a month after the funeral, life for the Maitlands was returning to normal. David was back at work; hospitals were always busy. Jon's driving lessons were under way with encouraging assistance from Chrissy who tested him regularly on the Highway Code, as well as keeping the home in order. Maddy was starting her A-level course and was already putting together her portfolio for the Fashion and Design course. Alex was spending time on the golf course, walking her dog (as if playing golf were not exercise enough!) and keeping her little garden tidy.

Gary, however, was not his usual self. Morose to the point of being downright miserable, even the nurses had noticed that the quips and banter with the patients had dried up. He spent a lot of time looking over his shoulder as though he dreaded what he would find following him. Until the day he was in A&E and a familiar voice greeted him.

'Sorry I'm late coming back for a check-up. I've been busy.'

'Oh, it's you.'

Gary was both worried and relieved to see Vince Spivey. Worried because he was sure that further demands were about to be made on him; demands which would probably take him outside the law; relieved because the waiting was over, he could stop looking over his shoulder, the bogey man had arrived. There was also a very faint hope that Vince would relent and go on his way without making any demands.

'How has the leg been. It's about a month now, isn't

34

which her father reckoned would break some boy's heart one day. Her school reports had always mentioned her conscientious attitude to work and she had accordingly done well in all her exams, with a crop of A's and A-stars to her name. In choosing Textile and Fabrics for A-level, her ambitions lay in haute couture on one side of the cat-walk or the other.

Maddy was the quiet member of the group. Her long brown hair hung like a pair of curtains to hide a pretty face. She had an excellent sense of humour which boded well for her other choice of A-level - Performing Arts. Even David and Chrissy were surprised that their quiet daughter could put in such an explosive performance in school plays. Her strong singing voice was going to be an asset if she achieved her ambition to get into the professional theatre. Textile and Fabrics was the other string to her bow – on stage or off, she would get into theatre.

Diminutive Suzy was a bubbly blonde. Universally popular, particularly with the boys, she would help anyone who was in need of it. She always had time for others, whether it was baby-sitting for new mums or shopping for senior citizens – she even took an old lady's cat to the vet for treatment. She wasn't brilliantly academic; she had to work hard to pass her exams, but enthusiasm, energy and her pleasant manner made up for any shortcomings. Not for her the bright lights and heady heights that Kelly and Maddy had in mind; she would be life, soul and mainstay of the village for many years to come.

'Found it!' Kelly had to shout over the music and turned down the volume before her father could come in and request a bit of quietness.

The dancing ceased and they spread themselves over the bed with the randomness of the following week's laundry having been flung there from across the room. Maddy drew back her long hair in an attempt to see the papers that Kelly was holding.

'You'll have to read it out, Kell, I can't read upside down,' she said and turned on to her back as if to emphasise the point.

'OK, here goes,' Kelly announced, in her best announcer's voice, 'Candidates should have an understanding of....'

'All right, Sophie Raworth. You're not reading the news now,' Suzy interrupted, 'Just read it so we can understand it.'

'That was the simple bit. Wait till we get further down the page. What's 'calendering' and 'delustering' and 'appliqué' and.......' she scanned down the page looking for other words that she had never met and didn't understand.

'All right, just give us the bare bones of it,' Suzy said

Kelly relented and picked out the headings. 'We've got Fitness for purpose, Finishes, Creative Techniques...'

'That will suit you, Maddy. You're very creative,' put in Suzy

'Use of sewing machines, Embroidery....' Kelly continued.

'My Gran would be good at that.' Suzy again.

'Suzy, will you stop interrupting. Here, you read it.' She handed the sheet to Suzy, who then read it quietly to herself.

'Don't worry, I'll read it after you Suzy' Maddy said with a knowing look and a resigned grin to Kelly. They were used to dealing with Suzy. 'Miss Bubbly' they called her. She

She ran. As she did so, the footsteps quickened, a hand reached out and clutched her shoulder.

'Hang on!'

It was Jon's voice.

'Hang on, Sis' he said again.

She stopped.

'You idiot. You frightened me.' and she thumped him on the shoulder.

'I'm sorry. I thought you'd recognised me when you turned round.' he explained.

'Not with headlights on. I couldn't see a thing.'

Amid apologies, Jon and Maddy walked up the drive, home.

'Where have you been tonight? Anywhere interesting?' Maddy wanted to know.

'Round and about the villages. Nowhere exciting. Gary's talking about going to Liverpool soon, but don't tell Dad. He'll only get twitchy about me driving through the Mersey Tunnel.'

'Are learners allowed to do that?'

' Yes, if they are 'competent and accompanied' I think is the term used. Gary says I'll be fine.'

'Rather you than me. It gives me the creeps to go through there.' Maddy shivered.

'I bet you'll want me to drive you to a gig at the Arena when I've got my licence,' Jon laughed, as they reached the front door.

EIGHT

Earlier that evening, as Maddy had been getting ready to meet Kelly and Suzy, Jon was preparing for yet another driving lesson with Gary.

'It's just for experience,' he had explained to David, who had expressed his doubts about letting Jon loose with Gary as his tutor. 'He's very good at telling me how to do things and what to watch for on the road ahead, joining traffic et cetera.'

'Well, all right. I agree, he's a good driver, but he can play fast and loose with the rules, sometimes. Watch your speed. He has been known to be adventurous and ignore speed limits.'

'So far he's only told me to keep an eye on speed limits. No question of ignoring them. The other way, in fact. 'Keep your speed down' is a regular instruction – you could almost call it nagging at me, even if I get anywhere near 30 in the villages.'

'Obviously he's a better driving instructor than I thought. So, go on, then. Enjoy yourself. Be careful.' David could not stop himself advising caution, it was in his nature.

Jon left the house and stood on the pavement outside, chatting to Suzy, who had arrived early. It was some minutes before Maddy came out, her long hair flying as she rushed down the path. The girls made their way to Kelly's house nearby as Gary's car turned into their cul-de-sac. Gary got out, vacating the driver's seat for Jon and made himself comfortable in the passenger seat. The L-plates were already fixed on the car.

'Right, away we go.' he said, and smiled with satisfaction as Jon went through all the routines of seat belt, engine starting and mirror checking. He wasn't to be rushed by Gary's attempt to inject a bit of urgency.

'Can you fasten your seat belt, please?' Jon asked, then, as Gary complied, he checked the mirror again and said 'Mirror, signal, manoeuvre' as he pulled away from the kerb.

'Well done. You remembered everything,' Gary said, 'Turn left at the end of the road. We'll have an evening in the country.'

'Driving in the countryside is sometimes better for learners than driving in town,' Gary explained as Jon drove carefully through village streets. 'There's narrow lanes for a start and you never know what you are going to meet. Dog walkers, and the dog is not always on a lead. Families out for a stroll can be a pain. They invariably split into two; Mum, one child and a push-chair on one side of the road and Dad, a child and the dog on the other side. You have to go dead slow to pass them because the kids and/or the dog decide to cross to the other parent at the last minute. If you meet wide machinery, like combine harvesters, you're looking for a gateway to pull into; then there's kids on ponies, lots of hazards for you to negotiate – so this is all good experience for you. Loose animals are the worst because you don't know what they're going to do. If you meet cattle, for instance, make sure you allow them plenty of room on both sides of the car.'

'But wouldn't I be better to go close to the hedge on one side to give them room to pass?' Jon asked.

47

'Not really,' Gary replied 'because they don't see traffic the same as we do. There's always one which will try to pass you on the other side and squeeze down between you and the hedge. Your door panels would be pushed in and your wing mirrors knocked off. Give them room and they'll give you as wide a berth as they can.'

They chatted on pleasantly as Jon took them from village to village without any problems whatsoever. Jon told Gary that he was undecided about his future. He was not as academic as his father had been, hence his 'year off'. However, this would not be twelve months of lounging about as David had thought, rather he would be looking for a job where he could make his mark, be of service, a real career. 'Dad suggested the Police. It's a possible, but Mum wasn't so sure as it's too dangerous on the front line. I don't fancy the armed forces. I don't think I could kill anybody. You and Dad were lucky. You had the brains to be doctors, but I don't think dealing with sick people the way you do is for me. Gran has been a charity worker; she even went abroad. That could be a possible.'

After an hour of driving, Gary felt it was time for a break and they pulled into the car park of The Wheatsheaf, a charming, black-and-white timbered country pub. It was a peaceful sunny evening, with bird-song and distant harvesting machinery providing a rural background. They decided to sit outside.

'What do you fancy?' Gary asked.

'Still orange will be fine. I'm driving.' Jon smiled, His voice was slightly louder than necessary to announce, for the first time in public, that he was enjoying his new-found status of 'driver'.

Gary vanished into the pub as Jon found a seat at one of the picnic tables on the neatly-trimmed lawn. There was not long to wait until Gary came out with a still orange for Jon and a coffee for himself.

'I thought you'd be having a pint of bitter. That's your usual, isn't it,' Jon asked.

'You're driving, I'm supervising, so neither of us has alcohol. I've seen the results of drink driving too often in hospital. Too many of them involving the morgue. There are times when I think that they are the lucky ones when I see young bodies smashed up and consigned to a life of pain and disability when they had so much to look forward to. So that's rule number one. Don't drink and drive.'

'I see what you mean,' Jon said, sipping his drink thoughtfully. The lesson had gone home.

'I know I have a regular pint or so at the Ram's Head,' Gary went on, 'but that's because I go each night, well, each night Sheryl's working, to walk her home. You never know, these days, how dangerous it can be on the streets at night, especially for a woman. So, I'm a regular at the pub but I'm not a heavy drinker. I have to work next morning so a clear head is a necessity.'

Jon could see the sense in this and went back to an earlier conversation. 'You said the country lanes are good for learning to drive. Is that true?'

'It is. Let's put it this way. How many times have you changed gear in the last hour?

Jon's mind went back, quickly, totting up over the journey. 'I don't know. Stop start at junctions, passing those horses, those tight bends, must be about a hundred, at least.'

'And – I know it can't happen – but if I took you on the

49

motorway, you could drive for an hour without changing gear once. All you would learn is driving in a straight line at speed. What you need is time in the saddle as they used to say when I was learning to ride. But we'll do some driving on main roads at the weekend because we'll be going up to Liverpool.'

'Liverpool? That's through the tunnel, isn't it? Am I allowed to drive through the tunnel on L-plates?' Jon's excitement showed on his face.

'Yes you can. The rules are that L-drivers are allowed if they are 'competent and accompanied', to quote the rules. So you'll be OK as I'll be with you.'

'Is there any reason for us to go there or is it just for experience for me?' Jon asked.

'I have an errand to run, so, to kill two birds with one stone, I thought it would be good experience for you.' He didn't add that he was responding to a request, if such it could be called, from Vince Spivey. If anything shady was going on, and if the police were involved, an L-driver would be less conspicuous and would be less likely to be stopped. He only had the postcode that Vince had given him. He wasn't sure what would be the next move. Would he be making a delivery or collecting money/ He didn't fancy the latter idea at all; people don't like parting with their hard-earned and he had no experience of debt collecting. Things could get rough. He hoped that Vince would have taken such inexperience into account and would have given him something straightforward to do.

As they finally pulled into the home cul-de-sac, they had covered many miles on country roads. The sun had gone down so they had used headlights for the latter part. More good experience for Jon. Gary was satisfied that Jon was becoming a competent driver and arranged to pick him up on the following Saturday morning for their trip to Liverpool.

In his headlights, Jon saw Maddy ahead, walking home. He braked, said 'Goodnight' to Gary, got out of the car and ran up behind his sister, who, having turned and been blinded by the lights, ran to escape the approaching footsteps.

'Hang on!' Jon called.

'Hang on, Sis!' he called again.

She stopped.

'You idiot. You frightened me,' and she thumped him on the shoulder.

'I'm sorry. I thought you'd recognised me when you turned round.' he explained.

'Not with headlights on. I couldn't see a thing.'

Amid apologies, Jon and Maddy walked up the drive, home.

'How did your evening go? he asked.

'Pretty well. Don't tell Mum and Dad. Kelly brought out a bottle of vodka.'

'And all I've had was a still orange. You're not drunk, though, are you?'

'No. I wasn't sure I would like it.'

'And what do you think about it now?'

'It's brilliant. But I think I'll go straight up to bed when we get in, to avoid any questions.'

'Make sure you don't have hiccups. That'll give the game away.'

'Don't worry. I'm not drunk.'

And she walked into the gate post. Before making her way steadily up to the front door.

NINE

'I thought I saw your mother at the hospital this afternoon,' David said to Chrissy, as he hung up his car keys. 'I could be wrong, though. The corridor was quite crowded and she was a long way off.'

'There are lots of little women with short grey hair,' his wife responded. 'Or she could be visiting someone.'

'I suppose so. I didn't have the chance to catch up with her. I was busy as it was.'

'She hasn't said anything about feeling ill, or anything. She's lost a bit of weight but I put that down to the golf. She's playing three times a week at the moment. She would have said if she was worried about anything.'

David changed the subject. 'I think Jon 's doing well with his driving. He always seems very upbeat about it.'

'Yes. Whenever I've tested him on the highway code he's done well.' Chrissy put in. 'Gary must be a good influence on him. He's keen to go out and Gary takes him to interesting places, it seems.'

'And you had misgivings about letting him go out with Gary.'

'I think we both did, but it seems to work.' Chrissy replied. 'Mind you, your face was a picture when he said they'd stopped at a pub the other night. It's not like Gary to drink coffee at a pub, though.'

'It's a good job he was winding me up or it would have been the end of driving lessons.' David was emphatic.

'Perhaps we ought to offer Gary something towards the petrol. He's never flush for money and I wouldn't care to make it awkward for Sheryl to balance the books.'

'Good idea. Could you do it? It would be difficult for me as we work together. I don't see him very often.'

'I'll ring him later and ask him to call tomorrow, on his way home.'

Gary responded to Chrissy's invitation the next day. It was 3 o'clock in the afternoon when he walked up the drive and knocked on the door. Chrissy was surprised to see him.

'I expected you much later, after you finished work,' she said.

'I finished early today. It's not every day I get ladies ringing me, asking me to call.'

Chrissy immediately felt uneasy. Was this one of his suggestive jokes or was he taking advantage of David's absence? She couldn't be sure. When she invited him in, she led the way to the kitchen; she thought the lounge would be too comfortable, too inviting.

'So,' Gary began, 'what service can I perform for a lovely lady today?' he asked with a lascivious look on his face and rubbing his hands together like the evil villain in a Victorian melodrama. Chrissy was still not sure he was joking.

'It's just that... David and I were talking, ... and ' she was struggling to say the right thing that wouldn't leave an opening for another remark 'we're so pleased that Jon's doing well with the driving, and we realise it's your car, so we …'

'…wanted to show your gratitude?' he finished her sentence. 'I'm sure we can think of something.' with that evil look again.

Chrissy rushed on, not giving him a chance to elaborate 'So we would like to pay for a tank of petrol. We are so appreciative of what you are doing. David doesn't have the time and, anyway, kids don't take instruction from their parents, do they? Will fifty pounds be OK?' She proffered a single red note, which he took slowly.

'Well, thank you. That's a big help.' He sounded almost relieved, as if this note solved a problem. Saturday's trip to Liverpool followed by wherever Vince had in mind to send him were uppermost in his mind. He wouldn't have to explain to Sheryl where his money was going. As if to cover up his relief, he went on 'Jon is an excellent driver. He's careful and follows instructions very well. Even from his Uncle Gary,' he laughed.

'It's a long time since he called you that. What was he? Five, six-years old?'

'Something like that. Time flies, doesn't it? Seems like only yesterday that you and David were getting married. That was a great night, the stag and hen night. The Ram's Head was still echoing next morning after us singing in there. We met up with the girls from your hen night and your minders walked off so I walked you to the nurses' home. You became my first patient after graduation when you tripped off the kerb and lost the heel of your shoe. I diagnosed a grazed knee. Yes, I remember every detail of that night. It was fun, wasn't it? Never to be forgotten.'

Chrissy shivered slightly at the thought of Gary examining her knee. Was his examination the cause of her subconscious distrust of Gary all these years? She was also remembering the details, so far as she could recall, but she couldn't get away from the question that had bothered her all her married life. Was now the time to ask Gary what had happened? She decided not and went on. 'Yes, it's all a long time ago now.'

'Married, two children. How old is Jon now? Seventeen? And you've been married – what- eighteen years?' He stopped and raised a quizzical eyebrow, as if waiting for Chrissy to make the connection and finish the sentence. She didn't. He carried on. 'I enjoyed the night at the Ram's Head. And after. So much to remember. A goodnight kiss at the bottom of that long staircase at the nurses' home. I'll never forget it.'

'A goodnight kiss? I don't remember,' Chrissy began.

'I'm not surprised. You were plastered. I'd be more surprised if you remembered anything about that night.'

Chrissy was encouraged by the thought that the goodnight kiss had taken place at the bottom of the staircase. That would imply that she and Gary had parted company at that point, well away from the nurses' home. But there was still the problem of who had undressed her and put her to bed. And hadn't Gary said, with obvious pleasure, that he remembered every detail? Everyone else had gone ahead. Eighteen years of worrying would be hard to erase from her mind.

'Hi, Gary. Didn't know you were here.' Jon bounced into the room.

Chrissy immediately relaxed; there was no need to continue with painful reminiscences.

'You're early,' she said.

'School's only part time these days, is it?' Gary quipped.

'Something like that. There's a teacher off sick so the head said our group could finish early today. We'll be breaking up at the end of the week anyway, so we're not missing anything. Summer holidays at last. Perhaps we can get some extra driving in.'

'You mustn't put on Gary like that. He has his work

to do. Hospitals don't have long summer holidays, you know.' Chrissy would prefer it if Gary was not so involved with her son, but she couldn't do more than a little gentle persuasion.

Gary could see that his conversation with Chrissy was at an end and made his excuses and made for the door. 'I'll pick you up on Saturday morning. Nine o'clock OK?' he asked/

'Looking forward to it,' Jon said as he closed the door and watched Gary getting into his car.

TEN

David had spent his morning dealing with his outpatient clinic. This was always his favourite day, as patients presented with a variety of conditions such as heart attacks, angina, abnormal rhythms and valve diseases. He was also familiar with the patients as they had all been to see him previously. The knowledge of their lives gave him an all-round picture of the person before him. Although it wasn't his specialty, paediatric cardiology had been part of his initial training and occasionally a child presented with a small hole in the heart or other complex health issues. It was the variety of the cases that made the outpatient clinic interesting. It was also tiring and he welcomed the break at mid-day.

He made his way to the staff restaurant on the second floor. There was no such thing as a rush hour at Aggies as the staff worked shifts and took a break when it was convenient. On some days there were some who took just a minimal break due to the pressure of work, snatching a cup of tea and a bite to eat on the hoof.

Today was a quiet day in the staff restaurant and David was choosing his lunch when Gary came in. They exchanged cordial greetings and Gary joined David at a corner table when they sat down.

David took a bite of his ham and cheese sandwich.

'I hear Jon's doing all right with his driving?' he said.

'Yes, he's becoming very confident. Always aware of what's about him. He'll make an excellent driver, I think.' Gary replied. 'He had a bit of a loss of concentration the other week, I think it was due to Alistair's funeral. He was very preoccupied for a couple of days.'

'Ah, he's missing his grandfather, we all are. Dad was a big part of our family life.'

'I remember the chat we had in the corridor. You were so worried about him being in pain.'

'That was the day he died,' David said.

'Wasn't it fortunate that you're a doctor?'

'How do you mean?' David started to bristle as Gary lowered his voice to a confidential whisper.

'Well, you know. We know how to deal with pain, don't we? Perhaps a touch extra of the pain relief. Morphine, I suppose?'

David exploded. 'Christ, Gary. What are you suggesting? I'd never do that!'

'Nobody would blame you. His pain was getting to you and you were in there alone with him at the end.'

David slammed down his tray on the trolley and made for the door. 'I'm not listening to this,' he roared and left, leaving the door swinging on its hinges.

The other diners went back to their lunches as the excitement was over. It's not every day you see two doctors having a row, especially when one of them was the normally mild-mannered Dr Maitland.

David's mind was in turmoil as he returned to his office. He told his secretary 'No calls.'; she recognised that he meant it from the curt voice and the lack of a 'please'. The slamming of the door was a further clue that her boss did not want to be disturbed.

It was half an hour later that he emerged to join the human race again, during which time he had gone over the

59

previous conversation with Gary on the day his father had died. Yes, it was true that he had been concerned about the pain his father was suffering but he was sure he hadn't given even a thought to helping him on his way. Certainly he had said nothing that could have been taken as a hint of euthanasia. He had sat with enough relatives of dying patients who had been in the same frame of mind as he had been, asking the same questions as the end drew nearer. 'Isn't there something you can do, doctor?' and the answer had always been in the negative. Palliative care was all they could offer. Palliative care and the company of his son was all that Alistair had had as he passed out of his mortal life.

Why would Gary even suggest this? They had always had a good relationship. Admittedly, Gary had spoken confidentially, as friends, though it was the most unfriendly thing he could have said. At least he hadn't shouted it out for all and sundry to hear. Has he expressed his thoughts to anyone else at the hospital, someone higher up? Rumours like this could ruin an unblemished career. David went pale at the thought of being struck off, the worst punishment a doctor could receive. He would have to have it out with Gary, but it should wait until he had calmed down. He was reluctant to have another stand-up row in public.

ELEVEN

Sharp at nine o'clock on Saturday morning, Gary arrived to pick up Jon for his lesson and what, unknown to Jon, was an errand for Vince Spivey. Chrissy came to the door to see her son off and managed a smile and a wave to Gary as they left. She didn't want to appear unfriendly. Gary busied himself with setting the sat-nav to the post code that Vince had given him and dropped the paper it was written on into the door pocket on the passenger side of the car as Jon pulled away from the kerb. 'That should get us to where we're going,' he commented. 'Now we can follow instructions; it will be good practice for you. 'At the T-junction turn right,' the metallic voice instructed.

'See what I mean?' Gary said as Jon complied. 'We'll be by-passing Chester and taking the A41 going north. You haven't had much experience of roundabouts out in the country lanes, so today's trip will make up for that.'

Jon was concentrating on the driving and acknowledged with 'O.K.'

He began to relax as he gained experience of following lane markings and arrows, to the extent that he replied to the sat-nav occasionally with 'I've already done that,' when he had pre-empted a lane change.

Gary was quiet for most of the time during the trip, partly so as not to upset Jon's concentration and partly because he was worried about the task that Vince was going to give him. He had plenty to think about. Vince had hinted that there was something not exactly legal in the errand, which was his main worry. Then his perennial worry about money forced its way to the surface. His bets had gone down again, so he owed Barry Meadows even more than when he had called at the betting shop. He didn't fancy dealing with Vera's rottweiler persona. Chrissy's gift paid for today's petrol and the balance was riding on a horse at Haydock Park. Little did Smart Chance realise the weight of the responsibility it would be carrying at 2.30 that afternoon; Gary's £20 would become enough to deflect the wrath of Vera and of Sheryl, whose patience was growing thin with Gary's gambling, if it won, but 20-1 was a long shot, particularly as it was based on a rumour Gary had overheard in Outpatients earlier in the week.

They proceeded up the A41 to Birkenhead, having by-passed Chester and made good time. The roads were clear. There were no football crowds – Everton were away to Newcastle and Liverpool were due to play on Sunday. Jon's grip on the steering wheel tightened as they approached the Mersey Tunnel, but his nerves relaxed as he got used to the different environment. They emerged into the city centre and followed sat-nav instructions until Jon said 'Jeez, look at that!' This was his first view of Goodison Park, home of Everton Football Club. 'It's like a big blue whale among the minnows,' as he compared the blue sides of the grandstands with the neat houses in the streets opposite.

'Keep your eyes on the road,' Gary warned, 'You need to concentrate in this traffic.'

'Yeah, OK.'

'That's a fair description, though,' Gary said, and went on 'We're nearly there. Two minutes according to the sat-nav,' He took out his phone and dialled, 'Two minutes' he said when Vince answered.

Vince was waiting on the pavement, still on crutches, as they pulled up alongside him. Gary got out and followed him into the house, telling Jon to stay with the car as he left.

'What's going on?' Vince asked. 'Who's the kid?'

'It's OK. He doesn't know anything. I've been teaching him to drive and I thought he'd be a good cover. Nobody's going to suspect an L-driver. So, what do you want me to do?'

'I can't drive with this boot on and Terry is otherwise engaged, shall we say? So you can do a collection for me. Your driver's going to get plenty of experience today.'

'Why? Where are we going?'

'Rhyl.'

'That's along the North Wales coast. It'll take ages,' Gary protested.'

'Just over an hour. You can drive on the way out. Give the young lad a rest. You'll have nothing incriminating on board. Then he can drive you home.'

'When I will have something incriminating on board,' Gary finished his sentence for him.

'Exactly. And what you'll have is about ten thousand pounds in cash. Use this case. It's got a hidden box on the sides and in the lid, the bottom would be too obvious. I've put a few clothes in as well, just in case you're asked to open it. There's no point in locking it. That would make it look suspicious.

'So when do I get it back to you? You surely don't want me to come back this way as well, do you?'

'No. I'm going to trust you. You're a doctor, after all. Do I recall you liked a bet?

Gary nodded, wondering where this was leading.

'Well, there's racing at Bangor next Tuesday. That's near your place, isn't it? You'll take it there. Terry will be there in the Beamer and you can hand it over to him at the end of racing in the car park. He'll have bookie's boards and stuff in the car, so if he's stopped, he's got the perfect excuse for having a pile of cash.'

'Right,' Gary said, sounding doubtful. 'But I'm not used to carrying that amount of cash.'

'Look on the bright side,' Vince went on, 'You'll have a day out at the races as well.'

'Until the next time.'

'Yes, well, I've been thinking about that. You're only doing this because I'm crocked at the moment. You shouldn't have said what you did about nurses, so I hope this teaches you something. I took it as an insult to my sister. And that little nurse was embarrassed. So, get this right and you won't hear from me again. Get it wrong and you will. Good luck, doc. On your way. Here's the post code. You're looking for Megan.'

Gary rejoined Jon, who was listening to the car radio. He entered the new post code into the sat-nav. They swapped seats and the sat-nav directed them through the Kingsway Tunnel then on to the M53 southbound, heading for the North Wales Expressway. It was turning into a long day out.

Vince had been right. Just over an hour later they arrived at the address where Gary expected to find Megan or, rather, she would have to find him. He got out of the car and stretched. His every sinew had tightened up while driving, either from sitting in one position for an hour or just nervous tension. Jon did the same. Gary had told him they were making a collection, no more information than that, to protect him from guilt. They looked up and down the street, but there was no sign of Megan, just a young mum pushing a pram down the pavement, ducking her head against the cold wind that blew from the sea. As she passed them, she said 'Are you Gary?'

'Er...yes. Are you Megan?' He couldn't hide his surprise.

'I am. Got something for you. Inside. Follow me,'

Her direct approach had taken him completely by surprise. She was a slim girl with blonde curls showing around the edges of the hood of her coat. Ripped jeans and boots completed the picture of a hard-up young mother, but her features bore a hard look on what could have been a pretty face.

'Jon, you wait with the car.' Gary said and followed Megan into the house.

'Are you taking the case?' Jon asked, and took it from the boot and handed it to Gary.

In its day, when Rhyl had been the playground for the miners of the North Wales coalfield, this house had been a respectable bed and breakfast establishment, but over the years the clientèle had deteriorated and now was run down and dilapidated. Inside, it was clear that Megan did her best to keep it tidy. The furniture, such as it was, was well-worn, there were no ornaments, there were no dishes in the sink and the floor was clean. Gary's assumption that she was a young mum was proved to be just that -an assumption- as Megan explained that she used the pram for delivering and collecting. It was excellent disguise for her operations and so far the cops hadn't cottoned on to the subterfuge.

'Good journey?' she asked, as though he was an old

friend dropping in for tea. 'Vince told me you were on the way.'

'Yes, thanks. He's very organised, isn't he. Keeping you informed and so on.'

'You have to be in his business. You never know when the cops are watching. Open your case.'

He did, and she walked in from the little kitchen with a supermarket plastic bag stuffed with money, fifties, twenties and tens with a smattering of fivers.

'There's about ten grand here. Make sure you look after it. Vince seems like a softie, but don't cross him. I crossed him once and look what happened to me.'

She pulled back the hood of her coat to reveal a scar on her cheek which her hair barely disguised. Gary went pale, not so much at the wound, of which he saw plenty at the hospital, but at the surprise of the revelation and the realisation that Vince could have done this in cold blood. He packed the suitcase hurriedly, hiding the notes in the side compartments and with a few sympathetic words to Megan, he left.

Jon looked over his shoulder at the case which Gary had hurriedly slung into the back seat.

'What's that, then?' he asked.

'Just some stuff that Vince wanted collecting. He's broken his leg and can't drive so he asked me to do it as a favour.'

'Must be worth collecting for us to spend a day travelling up and down.'

'It is to him, I suppose. Just some clothes from his ex-girlfriend. Now can you get this car moving without the questions, please?'

'Oo. Snappee' Jon intoned, surprised at the change in Gary's attitude.

'Get on with it,' Gary commanded and lapsed into silence as Jon pulled away, a silence that reigned until they passed Rhuddlan.

'We'll take the scenic route home. Forget the Expressway, it's boring. Go for St Asaph and follow signs for Chester.'

He hoped that Jon wouldn't query the change of route; he didn't need to explain that this was to avoid police attention. He had kept Jon in the dark about the details of their journeys so far and aimed to keep it that way. They were well past Chester before he said, 'If you're free on Tuesday, we could have a day at the races. How are you fixed?'

'I'm game. Where at?' Jon asked, hoping for a long drive to Worcester or Wetherby.

'Bangor-on-Dee,' was the reply.

'Not much driving to that one, then. It's only down the road.' Jon was clearly disappointed.

'Let's hope it's worth it, then. Financially, that is.'

He turned the radio on in time to hear the racing results from Haydock Park. Smart Chance had not lived up to Gary's faith in his abilities, having fallen at the last fence, leaving Gary's hopes of financial salvation buried in the mud of Haydock Park. Gary hoped for better luck on Tuesday.

TWELVE

'Sit down, nurse.'

Dr Michael Upton's desk was impressively empty except for a pad of writing paper and a pen. He obviously didn't have anything else to demand his attention and Nurse Dawn Evernden knew that the interview would be long and painful. The last six weeks had been a torment. She knew she should have reported the disappearance of the tablets but was afraid of being accused of misappropriating them herself. This Monday morning interview was a terrible way to start the week.

'I'm sure you are aware of the sad death of Nurse Susan Davies of Ward 4 last week,' he began.

'Yes. Suicide I believe,' she replied, whatever hopes she had of leaving here unscathed vanishing into thin air. She knew the direction this was going.

'Exactly. It was very sad. She was a valuable member of the team. Apparently, a bottle of Morphine tablets had gone missing from her trolley and she was afraid of being dismissed, or accused of stealing them herself. We all know how conscientious she was. It played on her mind, leading to her taking her life. She couldn't face the shame.'

Dawn averted her eyes. She knew what was coming.

Dr Upton went on, 'This weekend we had a complete audit of all the drugs trolleys on this wing and we found that the bottle in your trolley bore the label and serial number of the one issued to Nurse Davies. The purpose of this interview, then, is to give you an opportunity to explain how this came about,'

'I didn't take them. Not the ones out of my trolley. I admit I took hers but I didn't expect her to …' She couldn't say it, knowing that her actions had caused the suicide. It felt like murder.

'So, what did you do with the bottle from your trolley?'

'It was missing at the end of my shift. I don't know who took it, but it wasn't me.' By now she was very agitated as her raised voice showed.

'How long had you known about the shortage?

'It was about six weeks ago.'

'What? There is supposed to be a monthly audit of drugs. Why didn't it throw up the discrepancy?'

'On the day it was due, the Staff Nurse who usually does it was off sick.'

'But somebody else should have done it,' he said

'It was the day of the coach crash on the bypass and we had about forty injured pensioners all at once. I suppose the audit got forgotten.'

Michael Upton made a hurried note on his pad, and went on.

'You suggest someone else took the bottle. Did you have any ideas when it went, or who could have taken it?'

'No sir,' she said. 'I never leave my trolley when I'm on my rounds, or not normally, but...'

'But what?'

'There was one day when I took my eye off it for a minute or so. Doctor Maitland was having a problem with a patient, Ward 7, I think it was. The patient was suffering an angina attack and pulled his drip over so I ran to help. Doctor Maitland asked me to use the GTN spray to calm him down. But it was only for a minute or two. The trolley was by the ward door. The corridor was quite busy but I didn't see anyone near the trolley before or afterwards and I didn't notice that the bottle had gone. It was only at the end of my shift that I realised it had gone.'

'So you helped yourself to a bottle from Nurse Davies's trolley? With tragic results.'

'Yes, sir.' She hung her head.

'Very well. Nurse Evernden, I'm going to suspend you for two weeks. I will also have to notify the police to investigate, so you can expect a visit at any time. You had a promising career here and this unfortunate event will certainly make us think hard about what responsibility we can give you in the future, if at all. Go home now. I will have a copy of this interview typed up and sent to you. You should also get in touch with your union representative. You need all the help you can get.'

She repeated the morning's interview to Detective Inspector Nick Price when he called at her neat little flat in Chester that afternoon. By then, Dr Upton had sent a typed copy of his interview notes to her by courier. DI Price had taken a copy. Dawn felt that as she had told the truth she would have nothing to hide.

Nick began 'The fact that the tablets you took from Nurse Davies were all accounted for indicates that you were not stealing them to sell, but the fact remains that your original bottle of tablets has vanished. We are obviously concerned to keep drugs off the streets, so the question is, where did that bottle go? Who took it?'

'Not me,' she came back quickly. 'I don't know when it went or who would have taken it. I've had time to think since it happened and no-one has looked suspicious, nothing has ever been mentioned which would make me suspicious. The patients were mostly in their beds at that time apart from one or two in chairs and in that ward they were all very elderly. They'd never be able to get out of bed, steal the pills and get back into bed in the short time I was helping Doctor Maitland. Perhaps you ought to ask him if he saw anyone taking them from the trolley.'

'Don't worry, I will,' Price replied.

'And that was the only time my trolley was unattended, I returned it to the storeroom and locked the shutter at the end of my shift. That's all I know.'

'Yes, I can see that. We'll leave it at that for now. I might need to come back if anything else develops.' He left, leaving a distraught Dawn sobbing on the sofa.

DI Price rang the hospital and made an appointment to speak to Doctor David Maitland at 10am next morning.

He kept the appointment promptly, made his introduction and promised to be as brief as possible as the doctor was no doubt a busy man.

'I'm enquiring into the disappearance of an amount of Morphine,' he began.

David was puzzled. 'What is this to do with me?' he asked.

'Do you know Nurse Evernden?'

'Of course. But only on a casual basis. We both work here so our paths cross frequently.'

'Have you ever worked together?'

'Not really. She is in the pharmacy and I run clinics, so there is no need to work together, as you put it.'

'Sorry, you must forgive my lack of knowledge of how hospitals work. Do you recall an occasion when a patient pulled a drip over and needed attention?'

'Yes, a few weeks ago. Billy Welford, if I recall.'

'Would you like to tell me about it?'

'It was pretty straightforward, really,' David was confident. 'We don't get this happening on a regular basis. Billy, that's the patient, suffered from angina, a disease of the heart...'

'Yes, my father has it.'

'So there's no need for me to describe symptoms. As I was saying, Billy had a sudden attack. I had closed the curtains to commence my examination and he was thrashing about, one hand clutching his chest, the other waving in the air. He may have been trying to attract my attention, but, as I got to him he took hold of the drip and it overbalanced and fell to the floor with a crash and he would have followed it but I managed to hold him in bed. This took both hands so I called the nearest nurse to help me. Nurse Evernden had just turned into the ward with her trolley and she acted quickly. She ran to my assistance and I asked her to administer a dose of GTN, which immediately calmed Billy down. We straightened Billy and his bed out and when he was settled, we went back to what we were doing. And that was it. But I don't see how this fits in with missing morphine. Or Nurse Davies. That was very sad.'

Price decided not to correct David's leap to the wrong conclusion, connecting the mention of missing morphine to the unfortunate Nurse Davies, news of whose demise had gone round the hospital quicker than a virus.

'Did all the patients stay in their beds during this burst of activity?'

'As far as I can tell. One or two were sitting in chairs,

reading the papers or magazines, but nobody was up on their feet, they were too interested in Billy's problems – and mine, if it comes to that. It was a bit of relief from the humdrum routine of their day.'

'Did you see anyone come into the ward or go near Nurse Evernden's trolley?'

'I don't recall seeing anyone. I was too involved with Billy.'

'And did you, yourself, go to the entrance to the ward, near the trolley?'

'No. Not until I finished my rounds. By then, I recall that Nurse Evernden had also finished her distribution of drugs and the lid was down on her trolley as she left the ward.'

'And you're positive about this?'

'Of course. I have no reason to lie.'

'You do seem to have a very clear picture of what happened.'

'I can remember everything that happened that week. Every single detail. It was the week my father passed away in this hospital'

'I would have thought the reverse would apply, that your memory would have been overpowered by the bereavement.'

David decided not to argue any further and changed the subject. 'Tell me, why are the police looking into this? And what has Nurse Evernden got to do with it?'

'The missing drugs went from her trolley, not Nurse Davies's. She says she had taken those from Nurse Davies's to cover up the shortage in her own.' He stood up. ' Thank you for your time this morning. We may be in touch again.'

David sat and thought for some time before resuming his scheduled clinic. He had a lot to think about.

Nick Price made his way to the Admin Wing of the hospital. He hoped for a word with Michael Upton.

'Yes? Can I help you?' Dr. Upton's secretary answered Nick's gentle tap on the door as he entered.

'DI Price,' he introduced himself. 'Do you think I could have a quick word with Dr Upton, please? I'll be very brief. Just an update on the missing tablets.' He thought it wise to pre-empt any objections that the doctor was very busy by assuring her that he would not take long.

Following her quick phone call, he was shown into Dr. Upton's office.

'Good morning, doctor. As I was in the hospital this morning I thought I'd just give you an update. I was going to say 'progress report' but the truth is that there has been no progress so far. I have interviewed Nurse Evernden and Dr Maitland and their accounts of what happened in Ward 7 that day are identical. That can be suspicious sometimes, but I didn't think they had been rehearsed.'

'So, the search goes on,' Michael Upton observed.

'I'm afraid so. I understand that Dr Maitland's father died here in that week. Are you able to tell me the cause of death? Was there a post mortem?'

'Dr Alistair Maitland was well known to us at St Agnes' over many years and it was a matter of great sadness to everyone here when he was diagnosed with cancer. He had been an in-patient here for the last couple of weeks of his life and he died peacefully of that disease. I believe his son was with him at the time. There was no requirement for a *post mortem* in those circumstances. He was a very popular

GP. The church was overflowing for his funeral which was followed by a family service at the crematorium.'

Nick Price was impressed with this report, which not only answered his questions but also gave him further details which he hoped would be useful. He thanked Dr Upton and left. He made a point of thanking the secretary on his way out. He noted that her name badge said 'Helen'. He always kept on the right side of people with power, and secretaries had the power to open doors, even when their boss had instructed otherwise. Knowing her name may well open doors in the future. It had also not escaped his attention that she was a pretty blonde with a pleasant manner. He looked forward to his next visit to Dr Upton's office.

THIRTEEN

Gary had spent a nervous weekend since arriving home from Rhyl. The case of money stayed in the car, covered with a blanket, to avoid Sheryl's inevitable questions. He had slipped out once or twice each evening to check that it was still there. By Monday, he had convinced himself that Megan's valuation was only approximate – hadn't she said 'About ten thousand'?- so probably Vince wouldn't know if he had helped himself to a couple of fifty pound notes. On Tuesday morning, Vince was a hundred down, Gary was a hundred up. If his selections on the Bangor race card won he would, perhaps, replace what he had taken. Or perhaps he wouldn't.

Late morning on Tuesday saw him picking up Jon and driving off to Bangor-on-Dee. Half an hour later they were turning into the car park at the course.

'This is a real family course,' he explained as they got out of the car and stretched their legs. 'This bank is a natural grandstand so you can see the horses all the way round. Plenty of room for the kids to play about. Everything's close by, restaurants, bookies, toilets, not like the bigger courses. It's a day's march from the coach park to the course at Cheltenham, Wetherby's almost as bad. The down side here is that there's no shelter from the wind from the Welsh hills over there, but it's a very pleasant place to enjoy an afternoon's racing if the weather's kind.'

They strolled about the area, watching horses being walked around after a long journey in a horse-box. There were some having their travelling bandages removed prior to tacking up, others were already tacked up in readiness for the first race.

Jon was taking in all this new scene. He had never been to a racecourse, nor had he ever been this close to a horse and was amazed at the size of some of them and of the seemingly diminutive size of the grooms who led them around. The smell of leather and hoof oil as they passed was new to him, adding to what was becoming a memorable experience.

Gary was eager to place a bet and he gave Jon a brief description of how to place a bet, how the odds worked and how to choose which bookmaker with whom to place your bet. He showed him how to read the race card and how to use it to decide on your selection.

They each selected a horse in the first race. Satisfied that they had chosen a good horse, having seen them gallop past on their way down to the start, they placed their bets, Jon a couple of pounds each way (Gary had explained how that worked) and, with the benefit of Vince's hundred, Gary was brave enough to place ten pounds each way on his.

The excitement of the race got to Jon and he was jumping up and down as his horse led all the way up the final straight while Gary's made a poor attempt to clear the last fence and fell. An overjoyed Jon collected his winnings. Gary's only comment was 'Beginner's luck!' before he started to make his choice for the second race.

'Didn't you say we'd got to meet someone today?' Jon asked.

'Yes. A guy named Terry. After the last race. That's why I parked near the gate so he could find me. I've only ever seen him once at the hospital but I think I'll recognise him.'

Gary's run of bad luck continued throughout the afternoon, his hundred pounds dwindling down to next to nothing. Jon's winnings from the first race were sufficient to fund his modest bets for the rest of the day, with a few pounds left over.

The bars and restaurants emptied as the bulk of the punters left to place a final bet or to get a good position from which to view the last race. Terry had no interest in the racing. It had been a boring afternoon for him, watching punters getting excited, losing money, getting drunk, following a well-worn circuit from bar to toilet, to bookie, to course, watch the race and back to the bar to start again. Girls in short skirts were tottering about on heels that were not designed for walking on grass, spilling lager from their pint glasses as they tried to keep up with their menfolk. Terry thought that the heels were not designed for walking on anything at all as he watched yet another victim of the decking making an ungainly effort to extricate the heel of her shoe which had been trapped in the gap between the slats.

Time to get comfy for the trip home, he thought, and made his way into the now empty toilets. He had hardly reached the urinals when the door opened and two men followed him in.

'Hello, Terry. Nice to see you.'

'Eddie. Robbie. What are you doing here?'

Eddie had walked over to Terry. Robbie stood with his back to the door, holding it shut.

'Same as you, I would have thought. Except one of us is going home with a lot of money.'

'You had a winner, then?' Terry asked.

'No such luck. But you're here to collect some money. It had better come home with us.'

'You must be joking. It belongs to my boss and that's where it's going.'

'No way. Mick has his spies and they have said that you are picking up a case full of money, but you're going to let me collect it. Man in a blue car, they said. By the gate on the way out. We can do this the easy way or the hard way. If you let me tie you up and leave you in that cubicle, you could tell Vince that you were attacked…'

Before Eddie could finish his sentence, Terry had swung his fist at the side of Eddie's head, knocking him to the floor. Robbie rushed across and his poorly aimed blow hit Terry's shoulder and spun him round as Eddie got up from the floor, shaking his head. Robbie grabbed Terry from behind, with both arms around him as Eddie moved towards him. Before Eddie could strike, Terry lifted both feet off the ground and pushed them into Eddie's chest. Eddie went backwards as did Robbie from the recoil. Robbie's elbow struck the doorpost of a cubicle, which broke his grip. Terry, now released made for the door.

'Stop him!' Eddie commanded.

Robbie dived at Terry, bringing him down. Terry kicked out and broke Robbie's front teeth with his boot; Eddie reached over to take Terry by the throat but he squirmed clear. He got to his feet but both assailants were between him and the door.

'You shouldn't have done that,' said Robbie, spitting blood and fillings on to the tiled floor.

Terry launched himself at both men, swinging his fists at their heads.

Robbie ducked and lunged forward – Terry felt a sharp pain in his ribs, his head swam, his legs felt weak, he looked down to see blood running from a wound in his chest.

'You bastards,' were his last words as he staggered, his life draining out of him as he fell to the floor.

'Put that knife away,' Eddie said. 'I think you've killed him.'

'He was asking for it.'

'OK, shove him in here'

They dragged Terry into a cubicle, shut the door and made for the exit. The last race was coming to a conclusion as they ran to the car park.

Jon was overjoyed at his betting success as they sat in the car, waiting for Terry to find them. Gary was getting anxious. Cars were starting to leave the car park and it was clear that if Terry was in this stream he wouldn't be able to stop for more than a minute to transfer the case. At last, a blue BMW came along, the passenger window slowly going down as it approached. It stopped alongside Gary.

'You waitin' for Terry?' The Liverpool accent was clear. Gary didn't recognise the speaker.

'Yes. Where is he?'

'He's been held up. Vince asked me to collect it.'

Gary opened the boot and took the case out.

"I'm not sure about this. I ought to ask Vince.'

'Come on. We're wastin' time. There's a queue behind us.'

Almost on cue, some of the following drivers, anxious to beat the rush, sounded their horns which just added to Gary's confusion. The policeman on the gate waved energetically to move the traffic on. Gary opened the rear door of the Beamer and shoved the case in.

'Who shall I say picked it up?' he asked into the cloud of dust and exhaust smoke which flew up in the wake of the speeding BMW as it filled the gap in the traffic caused by the delay. There was no reply.

The journey home was silent. Gary was sure had lost ten thousand pounds of Vince's money. There would be retribution. Serious retribution. He recalled Megan's scar. Her words echoed in his head. 'I crossed him once and look what happened to me.' This was more than 'crossed him'. Vince's response didn't bear thinking about. On the other hand, perhaps the pick-up was genuine, but it was a slim hope. He just had that feeling. He turned the radio on. Perhaps music would drown his thoughts.

Ten minutes later Dolly Parton was halfway through her rendition of 'Nine till Five' when the announcer broke in with a news flash.

'Police have closed all roads around Bangor racecourse following the discovery of a body in the toilets at the course. It appears that a man in his thirties died from knife wounds. Investigations are going on. Nobody is allowed to leave the course.'

Gary wondered if that was Terry,' The only good news was that Vince would never know that Gary had borrowed a hundred pounds. It was small comfort.

Jon was mystified by events and wondered how to broach the subject. He decided on the direct approach.

'That was the case we collected in Rhyl, wasn't it? What was in it?'

'I told you, some clothes from his ex..'

'I'm not daft. You and Vince and Megan all treated it as though it was gold dust. So did the guys in that car. So tell me.'

'You'll be better off not knowing.' Gary was still protective towards Jon, though he understood the lad's feelings, 'But I'd better tell you. I had a problem with a patient and he blackmailed me into stealing some drugs for him. He also wanted me to collect some of his drug money from Megan in Rhyl. He had a broken leg, so couldn't drive himself. He felt that the police would have no suspicions about a learner driver; your L-plates came in handy as camouflage. So it was drug money in the case. Ten grand. His mate, Terry, was to pick it up from me by the gate after racing finished at Bangor but I think that those yobs in the BMW had knifed Terry and picked it up as you saw.'

'But he said Vince had asked him to pick it up,'

'I think that was to convince us that he was genuine'

'Perhaps he was.'

'That's what I was hoping until I heard that news bulletin. Now I'm even more convinced that they had killed Terry after beating the details of the pick-up out of him.'

'So we're in trouble?'

'In a word, yes. Big trouble.'

'And all this time I've been driving round collecting drug money and I didn't know it! I'm an accessory. And I thought you were my friend.' The enormity of his situation was slowly dawning on him. 'I'm in trouble with the police and in trouble with Vince. And I'll be in trouble at home when my Dad finds out. I've done nothing wrong. I thought I was just having driving lessons. You'll have to get me out of this somehow.'

Gary looked grim. 'First thing is, don't panic. Just keep your mouth shut and we'll deal with what happens when it happens.

Vince Spivey was settling down to an evening in front of the TV. He was fed up with the limitations of his broken leg. What had he got? Another three weeks with this boot on and he'd be free. A pack of lager cans in the fridge would keep him company this evening. His wife was playing bingo tonight so he could please himself what he watched. Strange that he hadn't heard from Terry. He should be back home by now and they'd be stuffing money under the floorboards in the back bedroom. Terry's lateness made him uneasy and the more he thought about it, the more uneasy he became.

A knock on the front door forced him to struggle up off the sofa, pick up his crutch – he was only using one, now - and make his way down the hall-way. On the way, he analysed the knock. It wasn't the merry rat-a-tat-tat that Terry would have done. This was the heavy knock of someone who was used to making himself heard over the television which would invariably be going full blast at this time of the evening in almost every house in the land, someone who meant to be heard and didn't intend to knock twice. He opened the door slowly, knowing that it wouldn't be the cheery 'Job done, boss', from Terry that he wanted to hear.

'Good evening. Mr Spivey, is it?' WPC Sandra Harper asked.

'Yes, it is. What's up?'

Sandra introduced herself and her colleague, PC Kevin

Collins. 'May we come in? We'd like a chat. About your car.'

Vince led the way down the hall and turned the television down. This looked serious.

'So what's this about my car? Has it been pinched?'

'No, we've got it safe.'

'You've got it? Why? What's happened?'

'It was at Bangor racecourse. It was the last car in the car park and there wasn't anyone there who was going to drive it off, so the local force thought that perhaps it had been stolen and abandoned. They traced it back to you through DVLA.'

'No, I lent it to my mate. He was going to the races and I lent him the car as a favour. I couldn't go myself.' He indicated his injured leg.

'Was your mate about five-eleven with short fair hair? Would he be wearing an Everton scarf?'

'That sounds like a police description if ever I heard one. Yes. That sounds like Terry. What's he done?'

'I'm afraid we have some bad news for you,' Sandra said. 'A young man of that description was found in the gents toilets at Bangor racecourse. He'd been stabbed. He was dead before the medics got to him. I'm awfully sorry to bring bad news.' She could see the colour draining from Vince's face. She waited patiently while he composed himself. He had obviously had a shock. That news, so unexpected, would have been a shock for anyone. She didn't realise, though, that this shock ran deep. Vince and Terry had been inseparable mates since junior school days. Terry and his sister Julie were left on their own when their single mum June had died young. Terry had been fourteen years old, Julie nineteen, so she moved in with her boyfriend and Vince's mother insisted that Terry move in with them. There were no other relatives who could have taken them in. It had been a happy arrangement, with both boys benefiting from each other's company. Julie's boyfriend, now her husband, had joined the RAF and was currently serving in Cyprus. Vince, when Sandra's questions continued, undertook to let her know of her brother's death. He also agreed to attend for the formal identification which would be at Wrexham. Sandra explained that as the crime had occurred in Wales, the North Wales Police would be investigating.

'Your car isn't part of the crime scene so you can have it back straight away.' She glanced at his broken leg. 'In view of that, we'll deliver it here for you.'

'Thanks for that,' Vince replied.

' We'll be in touch, Mr Spivey. Good night.'

They left Vince pondering his loss. What was it she said? In the toilets? That meant that he hadn't collected the money. Gary must still have it. There was no need to worry about that.

FOURTEEN

Vince Spivey and Mick Laggan went to the same school, Perton Street Junior, and were the greatest of friends, that is, until the age of eight, when they discovered that Vince favoured the blue of Everton FC and Mick definitely preferred the red of Liverpool FC. From then on, while they remained friends superficially, a fierce rivalry grew up between them. Whether the contest was academic or sporting, they had to beat each other. The weekly spelling tests as they went through school were as keenly fought as any mediæval duel. The Merseyside Derby was enacted every Wednesday afternoon, when football was on the timetable, with as much fervour as the Premiership matches were played at Goodison and Anfield twice a season. No one kept score, of course, and, truth to tell, if they had, the result would have probably been a tie.

On leaving school, Vince had joined the family taxi business and when his father retired, Vince had opened up new income streams. Supermarket pick-ups and a couple of school runs kept him busy each day and brought in the bread and butter. The jam came when he developed a lucrative connection with tour guides off the cruise ships, showing visitors the sights of Liverpool, the Three Graces, two cathedrals, the Cavern, of course, and the two famous football stadia, his beloved Goodison Park with a grudging acknowledgement of Anfield. Liverpool's ground was always the last visit on the way back to the ship and drivers invariably apologised that they were up against time so couldn't stop for their passengers to join the Anfield

Stadium Tour. Vince's entrepreneurship also led him into drug dealing. The taxis were an ideal cover for distribution around the city and deals were done inside the taxis, away from prying eyes and the ubiquitous closed circuit TV cameras. He had also developed a customer base along the North Wales coast. Seaside resorts meant young people; waiters, waitresses and reception staff from the hotels, fairground attendants and all the seasonal cooks and cleaners from the B&B's, who, together with the hordes of visitors each summer provided a source of income for which Vince was eternally grateful. His visits to collect the takings enabled the bonus of the enjoyment of riding his Goldwing along the A55.

His gentle nature was a front. While he seemed, initially, reasonable to deal with, his other side came out if he was crossed in any way. Megan was a case in point. Five years previously, she and Vince had been lovers, inseparable, together for life, it seemed. She knew as much about Vince's business as anyone and he trusted her implicitly. One night, during a session of particularly active and enjoyable sex, she breathed the words 'Ooh, Wayne.' It was a couple of weeks later that the local papers carried the story of Wayne Jeffers, a tax inspector, who had fallen to his death from a motorway fly-over on the M6. There were no witnesses. Megan dropped out of sight. No one saw her for weeks. She had worn a hoodie winter and summer ever since to conceal the hideous scars on her otherwise pretty face. She had sworn allegiance to Vince out of fear of further retribution, in return for collecting his money and sex on demand when he made his collections.

Mick Laggan had also gone into transport on leaving

school. From washing lorries for J R Simpson's fleet as a youth, he caught the bug of long-distance transport by listening to the stories of the drivers. He threw himself wholeheartedly into the business. By the time he was 19 he had his HGV licence and by his thirtieth birthday he had visited every country in Europe; he had a smattering of French, German and Spanish, and he had come across useful contacts for some of the illegal activities which are facilitated by long distance travel. Old man Simpson had gone on too long, well past retirement age, and the business had deteriorated; latterly, just fifty miles radius covered all they had to travel. This suited Mick. When Jack Simpson finally called it a day, Mick was able to purchase a run-down business cheaply, knowing the potential it held for him in the future. 'Laggan Logistics' became as well-known a name on the motorways as Eddie Stobart's.

The down side of Mick's success was the lack of a Mrs Laggan. He had spent so much time on the road that there had been no room for long-term relationships, just a few girl friends here and there. Generally, the women he met worked in the offices of customers with whom he made contact when checking in and they became a useful source of bed and breakfast at the cost of a meal out at the local pub. He had a sister who had married and gone to live in Llandudno some years ago. At one time, he had paid her the occasional visit when he had a delivery in North Wales, but his visits had tailed off as he did less driving and more admin work due to the growth of the business. Added to which, he needed to keep his finger on the pulse just in case of a visit from the police if one of his illegal cargoes had been apprehended. He kept his fingers permanently crossed that this would never happen.

He also liked to keep tabs on Vince Spivey's activities. The old rivalry had not abated with time. Keeping ahead of Spivey's Taxis was still important to him. He knew that Vince was running drugs into the estates but resisted the temptation to point this out to the police, partly from the complicated friends and rivals relationship they had and partly (and more importantly) the fact that Vince knew about his illegal passengers – immigrant workers who he brought from the arable farms in the south and east of the country to work on the fewer, lesser extensive, arable farms, market gardens and abattoirs in Cheshire and Lancashire.

Vince's phone rang and flashed up the name of the caller.

'Evening, Mick,'

'Evening, Vince.'

It was almost as if Mick was lost for words with something to say but nothing to say it with.

'Did you want something, then?' Vince broke the silence.

'Don't know how to put this, Vince, but I have a case of your dirty washing here. And other interesting contents.'

Vince's blood ran cold. So Gary didn't have the case after all. 'How on earth.....?' he began.

'My boys were at Bangor Races today...' He got no further.

'The police have already told me what happened. It sounds like something Slug and Slime would do.' He mentioned two of Mick's men, so nicknamed because where one went the other was sure to follow

'Come on, Vince. Let's have a bit of respect for my lads.

I liked Terry. We were all in school together. I know Eddie and Robbie can be a bit hot-headed from time to time.....'

'So they've stolen my case and had to kill Terry to do it?' He was near to tears and filled with rage at the loss of his mate and finding out that it was at the hands of those two morons made it worse.

'He was very loyal to you from the fight he put up, so they told me. But he wasn't being co-operative, Vince. They asked him nicely but he started swinging his fists. It was the only way they could stop him.

'Asked him nicely, my arse. It's plain robbery. We've always had a good relationship, Mick. What's brought this about?'

'Well, it's tit for tat, Vince.'

'Why, what have I ever done to you? Live and let live seemed to work, didn't it?'

'It wasn't what you did to me, Vince. It was to my niece. That was a terrible thing to do.'

'What do you mean? I don't even know your niece.'

'Yes you do, Vince. Her name is Megan and she lives in North Wales. A pretty girl, she was, until you scarred her for life. Your money will set her up comfortably somewhere else. You'd better find someone else to collect your money. Sorry about the short notice.' He cut the connection.

'Hang on. .' Vince said to the empty air. Mick had gone and so had his money.

Sitting there alone he realised that he'd been set up by Mick and Megan. Bitch. He should have slit her throat while he was about it.

FIFTEEN

Alex Chisholm walked into St Agnes' Hospital and made her way to the Oncology Department. It was a familiar journey which she had made four times in the previous twelve months. She was careful to avoid an accidental meeting with David, whose office was at the other end of the long corridor which was the spine of this massive building. All departments and wards led off this corridor like ribs attached to the spine.

She had noticed her weight dropping from week to week; she had a suspicion that Chrissy had noticed but nothing had been said so she let sleeping dogs lie. She was not one for gushing sympathy and following Alistair's death she was reluctant to throw the family into further distress so soon. When the time came it would be soon enough to tell them.

She arrived at the Oncology Department and gave her name and date of birth to the receptionist. There was hardly time for her to warm the waiting room seat before the consulting room door opened and a middle-aged nurse asked her to go in.

'Mrs Chisholm. You're not related to Chrissy Chisholm by any chance?'

'She's my daughter. Do you know her?'

'Oh yes, we trained together, many years ago. How is she?'

The small talk was cut short by the arrival of Jim Parton, a pleasant man in his fifties, and Alex managed to get in 'If you see her, please don't say you've seen me here. I don't want her to know yet.' before following the

91

consultant into his office.

'Have a seat, Mrs Chisholm.' He invited. 'Would you like a cup of tea while we chat?'

'Will I need one?' Alex smiled and said 'Yes, please' before he could answer.'

Jim's secretary was given the job of supplying the beverage, which she did swiftly while Jim and Alex engaged in small talk.

Alex had been a prominent member of the Friends of Aggies She had organised a lucrative Golf Tournament each year for the last ten years, boosting the hospital's funds and therefore its capability to give swift and effective treatment to all its patients. She always attended the smaller events, car boot sales and coffee mornings which kept money flowing into the coffers

The tea arrived and the conversation turned to the reason for her visit.

Jim asked how she felt and checked on any changes since her last visit. 'I'm sorry, but the news is not good. This latest x-ray shows that the cancer has grown and is virtually inaccessible without an operation. Radiotherapy and/or chemotherapy would reduce your quality of life and are unlikely to be totally successful. It is so advanced, I'd say that the operation and its aftermath would give you more pain than if we left it alone. I'm afraid we are reduced to offering palliative care. I'm sorry to give you such news. We'll inform your GP and she will organise your treatment from now on. Rest assured that we'll do all we can to smooth the path for you.'

'Thank you, Jim, for being so honest. I'm going to have to live with it, I suppose. Can I ask – how long have I got?'

'It's always hard to be accurate, but I would say weeks rather than months. I'm sorry.'

'Can I ask that you don't mention this to Dr Maitland if you happen to see him. I want to tell the family in my own time.'

With Jim's assurance, she left. Her tears would wait until a private moment at home.

The phone in Gary's office rang. 'Hello, Doctor Baker speaking,'

'I'm glad of that.' The familiar voice with a slight scouse accent struck fear into Gary's heart. He wanted to put the phone down, to close the whole sorry business; he wanted the earth to open up and swallow him, anything to avoid the inevitable conversation he was about to have.

'You made a mistake, giving my money to a stranger,' Vince opened slowly, not raving, not angry, just business-like, as Gary relaxed slightly.

'I'm sorry about that, it was very confusing. He was in a queue of traffic leaving the racecourse and he had to keep moving. All the cars behind him were blowing their horns. The policeman at the gate was waving him on.'

'You didn't have to give it to him.'

'If I argued with him the policeman would have come across to sort us out. What would I say? 'He's taking ten grand of drug money off me?' And what if he was genuine and I hadn't given it to him. You would have thought I had stolen it. I saw what you did to Megan so I didn't want that to happen to me.'

'I said to give it to Terry.'

'Well, this guy said Terry had been held up and you had

asked them to collect it.'

'That was a pack of lies.'

'How was I to know? It was all so rushed, so confusing. He wouldn't give me his name. He just drove off.'

'So, you owe me ten thousand pounds, Doctor Baker.'

Vince was stinging to think that Slug and Slime of all people had put one over on him to the tune of ten grand. The fact that Mick had put one over on him by setting him up with Megan added to the hurt. Five years and he hadn't had a clue. And there was a time when he thought he and Megan were becoming an item. Mick Laggan would literally be laughing all the way to the bank or wherever he was stashing his money these days.

'Where will I get ten thousand pounds from?' Gary asked, incredulous that Vince could even contemplate the idea.

'It's your problem. You could supply me with some more of those pills or do more deliveries for me. Over a period, of course.'

'I can't do that. There's a big investigation going on here over the last ones you had, so security is tightened up. And doing regular journeys to North Wales would be suspicious after a while.'

I can see we'll have to have a chat; face to face, if you see what I mean. I'll be seeing you.'

The phone went dead and Gary was left to wonder what Vince had in mind. When would Vince be coming? What did he mean 'face-to-face'? Megan's scars swam through his memory. How could he find enough money to satisfy his torturer? Gary put the phone down as the possibilities buzzed around his head like a swarm of angry bees. He would get no sleep tonight – or any night in the foreseeable future.

Gary's mind settled where it always did when he was considering his finances – or lack of them. A big winner was round the corner. His luck would surely change; his losing streak must come to an end soon. It was always more galling when he heard of other punters' successes, like the guy who won £250,000 for a £5 accumulator. The publicity this received carried no mention of the hundreds, or was it thousands, of accumulators which went down the drain each day. What could he do with quarter of a million just now? And now, to add to the pressure, Vince was threatening God knows what to get his ten grand back. It wasn't as though it was Gary's fault. He had handed it over in good faith, as ordered. How was he to know the guy was lying about Terry's absence? There was no way he could have known he was being robbed. He wasn't familiar with the car. Perhaps if he had been part of Vince's gang in Liverpool, he would have recognised the car as belonging to a rival outfit. Surely Vince could see that? The thought of a winning bet, a big winning bet, offered a bright ray of hope on the horizon. He would call on Barry Meadows and beg for more credit. His system would surely pay off this time.

It was with determination tinged with more than a touch of trepidation that he entered the betting shop on his way home. Late afternoon was a slack period so there were no other punters about. Vera looked up from cashing up her till as Gary's footsteps echoed on the tiled floor of the empty shop.

'Is the boss free for a word?' he asked.

'I think he spoke his last word to you when you called in

before,' Vera replied. She had a pretty good idea what it would be about and Barry had instructed her not to give any more credit to Dr Baker.

'But can I see him, please?' He realised he was begging and tried to hide his desperation.

'You'll be wasting his time and yours.'

'I'll take that chance...'

The office door opened and Barry appeared, carrying a bundle of betting slips.

'Can you check these....' he spotted Gary 'I'll be with you in a moment'

'Just asking for two minutes. I know you're busy but I'd like a word -' he glanced at Vera. ' - confidentially. Just a couple of minutes.' The words came out quicker than he intended. Desperation was beginning to show.

'Well, two minutes it is. Come into the office.'

He handed the slips to Vera with a brief instruction as to what to check, then unlocked the door at the side of the counter and let Gary through. The look on Vera's face, stern, unsympathetic, didn't do anything for Gary's courage. Obviously, she was not in agreement with any further chances for Gary, despite her confidence in him as a doctor.

'Close the door,' Barry said, but did not offer a seat.

Gary looked around the office. This was the first time he had been into the sanctum sanctorum. The computer and the screens which blinked around the walls seemed out of place, visitors from the 21st Century in an office which would have been modern a century and a half ago. Ebenezer Scrooge would have been at home here. A heavy wooden desk, leather-topped with pedestal drawers down each side stood at one end of the room and brown cupboards, a brown wooden filing cabinet and solid wooden shelves stood around the walls, looking as if they would have continued to stand there even if a bomb had demolished the rest of the building. From his seat in a chair which had probably been behind that desk since time immemorial but had been brought up to date with a swivel base, Barry could see all his screens; two screens for CCTV in the shop and outside kept tabs on everything that happened in his empire including information from a little camera above the till of which even Vera was unaware; Racing UK relayed course information on the next; yet another screen kept him informed of odds with other bookmakers online. He had seen Gary arrive and was pretty sure why Gary was calling. He had decided that this would be the time for a final warning.

'I'm finding this a bit embarrassing,' Gary began, 'but I've run into a bit of money trouble.'

'So what's new, Gary? You've always got money trouble. You owe me...' he pressed a couple of keys on his keyboard, 'nine hundred and sixty pounds at the moment. You've really overstepped the mark this month. I've told you before, I'm not a bank or a charity. I think I might call in at the Ram's Head on the way home and have a word with Sheryl. Perhaps she can reduce the debt.'

'No, no. Don't do that. Please. She doesn't know that I haven't paid you. I'll pay it at the end of the month. Pay day. Honestly.' he lied, hoping he would be able to keep it from Sheryl. So many domestic bills were unpaid he was drowning in a debt which even a doctor's salary was struggling to cope with. No longer was he robbing Peter to pay Paul. He would have to rob all twelve disciples and more to solve his problems. He went on, 'The trouble is, there's a guy in Liverpool reckons I owe him ten grand, it's a long story, and a big win is the only way I can see out of it, just to keep him happy. He's a dangerous man, and violent.'

'How on earth can you owe ten grand?'

'I said it was a long story, but basically, I was delivering a case with the money in and I gave it to the wrong person. It wasn't my fault. I don't know these people. So I'm asking you. Please, fifty pounds credit. I've got a tip for tomorrow at Haydock. It hasn't run for two months so it's going to be fresh and it'll be long odds.'

'You've got this all wrong, Gary. Assuming it wins, why would I give you the winnings to give to someone else when you already owe me money? You're not logical. This has gone on long enough. I want my money at the end of the month as promised. If I don't get it, there will be trouble. The guy in Liverpool isn't the only one with a way to settle debts. And there'll be no more credit. So goodbye, Gary. Till the end of the month. Close the door on your way out.'

Gary had always thought of Barry as a gentle little man, but seeing the steel behind his words worried him as much as Vince's phone call. He left without a word, not even a goodbye to Vera as he went through the shop. Where would he go from here?

SIXTEEN

DI Nick Price smiled at Dr Upton's secretary. ' Hello Helen. I don't need to see Doctor Upton, but I thought I'd better let him know that I'm conducting enquiries in the hospital at the moment. Perhaps you could do that for me?'

'Yes, certainly,' she said, returning the smile. 'Thank you for telling me.'

'Before I go, could you tell me who would have been responsible for checking the drugs trolleys. I'm not used to hospital ranks and duties, as you can see.'

'There's a Staff Nurse in charge of the Pharmacy. That would be Nurse Janet Neville. She will be in the Pharmacy now, if that's any help.'

'It is, thanks very much.'

She gave him directions to the Pharmacy, which was well sign-posted once you got to the central corridor and he left. Amazing what a 'thank you' to the secretary on his first visit had achieved.

He arrived at the Pharmacy in time to find Janet Neville recording the results of her latest check of drug trolleys. He introduced himself and told her that he was investigating the loss of the drugs.

'Well, I was away on the day the audit should have been done,' She was defensive and tried to absolve herself of any blame.

'I'm not accusing you of anything,' Nick said. 'If the hospital feel you should have checked whether it had been done when you returned to work, that is their problem, not mine. I'm trying to find out where and when the drugs went six weeks before. So, first of all, I'd like you to help me understand the procedure for issuing drugs.'

She felt immediately relaxed to hear that she was not suspected of anything, though the threat of action following the oversight that the policemen had pointed out was still a worry. She had a sticky interview with Dr Upton coming up.

'Well, prescriptions from the wards come in via the internal post or sometimes directly in urgent cases. The nurses sort them and load up their trolleys. I physically check them before they go out. At the end of the day, the trolleys are parked in here and the shutters pulled down on the trolley bay. Nobody then has access to the trolleys. There is a nurse in here 24/7 to issue drugs in case of emergencies.'

'But does anyone check the trolleys when they return?

'Only the nurse who has taken it out.'

'So how would you suggest the pills from Nurse Davies's trolley got into Nurse Evernden's?'

'The individual trolleys are not lockable. We've always considered the shutter lock is sufficient security. Obviously it isn't. If Nurse Davies had gone off shift, Nurse Evernden would have easy access to all the trolleys.'

'Thank you for that. It seems a straightforward system. Just a few tweaks in your security will stop this happening again. I can leave you in peace. Did I see a sign for a restaurant on site? I'm ready for a break.'

She directed him to the staff restaurant and went back to work a relieved woman.

Nick found his way to the central corridor and followed signs up to the staff restaurant, where he ordered a Latte and a Danish pastry. He knew the public restaurant would be heaving, it always was. There were very few customers in the staff restaurant at this time of day. Good decision. He chatted to the waitress as his Latte went through its procedures.

'This must be a pleasant place to work. No pressure. Nice customers. No hassle.'

'Yes, I suppose so. We have our moments, though, like anywhere.'

'Such as?' he asked.

'One of the doctors orders Apple Crumble for lunch, every day. One day, he was delayed and one of the new girls sold the last one before he got here. She wasn't to know but he took it personally. He was raving at the manager for half an hour. Wanted her sacked, but it didn't happen.'

'So these doctors are not always the calm individuals that we imagine them to be?'

'Oh, no. There was a big blow up one day. I don't know what it was about. But Doctor Maitland was shouting at Doctor Baker and stamped out of here in a real strop.'

'Really? That's interesting.'

Nick knew where he was going for his next interview. Choice of two.

SEVENTEEN

Who to visit first? That was the question in Nick's mind as he rejoined the central corridor. Maitland was upset by what was said. Therefore, was there some kind of accusation by Baker? Logic said interview Baker first, he seems to have nothing to hide. Maitland might be less than forthcoming, if the accusation were true. Nick wondered what the accusation was, how serious was it? He used his mobile to ring Dr Maitland's secretary and made an appointment for later that morning, then arrived at the General Surgery department. The receptionist here confirmed that Gary was in and available for the interview.

Nick was surprised to find that the office was just like any other – just a few papers on the desk, the ubiquitous computer screen, a few reference books on the shelves, no real indication that there was any medical connection whatsoever.

'Have a seat,' Gary offered. 'Sorry, we don't run to teas and coffees down here.'

'That's fine,' Nick replied 'I don't think this will take long. I'm investigating the missing tablets. I'm sure you've heard of them?'

'Yes. Talk of the hospital, though we've managed to keep it out of the press, I believe.'

'So far, anyway. Have you any thoughts on how they were taken?'

'Not really. They are always in the trolleys and they are locked up at night, so I have no idea how they could have gone.'

'How do you get on with Doctor Maitland?'

'That's a bit out of the blue. What's that got to do with the missing tablets?'

Nick avoided the question.

'It's just that I believe you had a bit of a run-in with him in the restaurant a few weeks back.'

'Yes. I wasn't really serious but he took it personally. I've known David for years. We were at medical school together and I know his family well. I was Uncle to their kids when they were little. I'm teaching his son to drive. We get on well.'

Nick wasn't to be diverted by a change of subject.

'So what was the row about. He must have been very upset if you are as close as you say you are.'

'We spoke in the corridor one day about his father who was very ill, in this hospital. He was worried about the pain the old man was suffering, frustrated that we could do nothing about it, even as doctors. I think it was about then that the tablets went missing. David's father passed away that afternoon and David was alone with him as he went. I wasn't serious, I just mentioned the way things had gone. He took it as an accusation and blew his top.'

'But it was highly unlikely – a respectable doctor,' Nick suggested.

'Well, it happens, doesn't it? I bet Dr Shipman's patients thought he was respectable until he got found out. You never can tell.'

'I suppose not. If it was always clear-cut, I'd be out of a job.'

There was nothing else to ask at this stage. Nick closed the interview.

'Thank you, then. I'll be on my way. I don't suppose I'll

need to see you again.'

'Glad to be of help,' Gary said, feeling confident that he had successfully deflected attention away from himself as he closed the door.

Dr Maitland's office was a replica of Dr Baker's, Nick found as he walked in. No charts or posters of the human skeleton on the walls. These doctors would know it all by heart. No need for reminders. He found David Maitland to be a calm, well-mannered person who seemed a little surprised to be interviewed again by Nick Price.

'How can I help?'

'I'm still investigating the missing tablets,' Nick began. 'As you can imagine, morphine has a certain street value, so a robbery like this is serious and has to be investigated.'

'I agree, but I don't think I can shed any further light on the matter.'

'I believe you had a disagreement with Doctor Baker in the restaurant a few weeks back. What was that about?'

'It was just something he said, or perhaps the way he said it that I didn't like. Something and nothing, as they say.'

'It didn't sound like something and nothing to me.' he referred to his notes. ' You were shouting at Doctor Baker and went out in a real strop, as someone described to me. What do you think of Doctor Baker?'

'I've known him a long time, we were students together. I wouldn't want to speak badly about him but it's well known that he likes a bet which has caused money troubles in the past. He's familiar, perhaps over-familiar, with females, nurses and patients alike, but he's popular as a result. He's a family friend; he's teaching my son to drive, for instance. Just an ordinary fellow with ordinary problems, as far as I know. I probably blew up because I was having a rough time after losing my father. Bereavement does that, you know.

This didn't fit with Dr Maitland's previous statement that he could recall everything that happened that week; Nick was immediately suspicious. He would press on. Perhaps a more provocative question would prove fruitful.

'Could he have suggested that you had used your position to ease your father's pain?'

David paused, taking a tight hold on his temper. He replied in a quiet, deliberate voice

'It was something like that but I refute any suggestion that I would steal tablets or perform euthanasia, especially with my own father. If anything along those lines appears anywhere outside this room I shall be consulting my solicitor and I'll sue. I have too much to lose from such idle speculation'

Added to the professional disgrace; he would not wish for his family to hear even a hint that he had assisted his father out of this world. The loss of their respect would be devastating.

Nick made notes. He wasn't convinced either way. If Maitland had performed euthanasia he was hardly likely to admit to it on the first suggestion of his guilt. On the other hand, his vehement denial and threat of legal action could be a genuine reaction indicating his innocence. Or was it? More evidence would be necessary before he could decide. It didn't help that the body had been cremated.

When David arrived home that evening there was a letter on the kitchen table, unopened.

'What's this, then?' he asked Chrissy, who shook her

head.

'I didn't like to open it. It looked so...so... ominous. It had been pushed through the letter-box while I was out at the shops.'

It certainly had an odd look about it. The envelope itself was just plain white, no franking marks. No indication of the sender, no 'return in the case of non-delivery' address. Nothing odd so far. But the inscription on the front was indeed ominous. The words 'To whom it may concern' were not in handwriting or typing or produced by a computer. The letters were individually cut from a newspaper in differing fonts and sizes and glued to the envelope' obviously intended to hide the identity of the sender.

Jon and Maddy bounded noisily into the room, having had an afternoon at the bowling alley in Chester, their boisterous laughter immediately silenced by the serious demeanour of their parents.

Jon found his voice first. 'Has something happened?' he asked.

His father nudged the envelope round so that Jon could see it and read the inscription right way up.

'Just read it, but don't touch it,' David instructed. 'If it's serious, we don't want our fingerprints to make it any more confusing. Fingerprints may be the only way we can identify the sender.'

'It's somebody having a joke. Probably telling us we've won the lottery or your rich long-lost Uncle Albert has just arrived from Australia and wants to give us his gold mine.'

'We're not sure who it's intended for,' Chrissy put in.

Maddy, for her part, remained quiet. Practical jokes were

going around in school. Entries on Facebook, invitations to non-existent reunion parties – what if Suzy hadn't deleted the photos and someone had got hold of them? Could this be the publicity she dreaded?

'We'll have to open it,' her father decided, have we any latex gloves?

'I'll get some from the kitchen,' Chrissy said and left the room to return with gloves and a knife with which to open the letter.

'You'll need this,' she said, handing David the knife and he proceeded to open the letter with the care of a surgeon doing a heart operation. He was leaving nothing to chance. He unfolded the letter and laid it on the table so they could all read it.

To whom it may concern.
You know how you did wrong.
I know too.
And I know how your family will react when I tell them.
So do you.
So think about how we can keep this quiet.
It will not be cheap.
I'll be in touch.

Silence was palpable as the whole family searched their memories, each finding something worth hiding. The silence was broken by David.

'This must go to the police,' he said, starting to gather up the letter, but Chrissy stopped him.

'Just a moment, let's take a look at it. We haven't had time to digest it yet. It doesn't mention the police, it's only revelation to the family.'

'Mum's right. Whatever it is, it's only a family matter.' Jon was with Chrissy all the way.

Maddy was more analytic. 'But it also says 'It won't be cheap.' That means the next note will be a blackmail note.' Her conclusion was in tune with David's view. This was serious enough for police action.

David, ever cautious, had second thoughts. 'We'll sleep on it. You never know, it might be a hoax. Let's see what happens next.'

EIGHTEEN

DI Nick Price approached Dr Upton's office. His winning smile was returned by Helen as she confirmed that he could go in to see her boss. Dr Upton, in his turn, was equally pleased to see the policeman, to whom he offered a seat and a cup of coffee, then rang through for Helen to provide two Americanos.

'Good morning, Inspector. This is a coincidence. I was about to ask Helen to ring you to ask you to call in to see me and here you are.'

'Yes, I thought I would give you an update on the missing morphine. Shall I go first?'

'Yes, please. My news can wait.'

'Very well. First of all, no trace of the tablets has come to light, but I think we could have expected that. Whoever took them will have taken them out of the hospital and on to the streets as soon as possible. As regards a suspect, I think that Dr Maitland is still in the frame. Unfortunately, his father's body was cremated, so there is no way we can find out whether euthanasia was involved. The weakness in our case is that, if that was why he had stolen the tablets, what has he done with the unused ones? I assume a couple of tablets only would have been sufficient to ease Maitland Senior out of this world, but there were a hundred in the bottle. It looks as though we might be relying on a confession before we can charge him with anything. The case against Dawn Evernden is very weak and I think she can be eliminated from the enquiry. If she had wanted to steal the tablets, why not just take them from Nurse Davies's or any other trolley. The cover-up was entirely unnecessary; it makes no sense at all. I must say that I am surprised by the latitude you give to nurses like Dawn Evernden. They have access to controlled drugs, there are no checks of trolleys at the end of the day, and a monthly audit is far too late if any similar problem arises in the future. That's as far as I have gone. Perhaps another interview with Doctor Maitland will be fruitful. I will set it up when he is next free.'

He sat back as Liz, Helen's young assistant, brought in the coffees and placed them on the desk. Dr Upton took a sip of his and waited for Liz to leave the room.

'That's a very comprehensive report. I can agree with everything you say, though I have my doubts about Doctor Maitland's guilt. He is a well-respected doctor. He is one of our rising stars here at St Agnes's, a top cardiologist and a personal friend to many of us. I would be very surprised if he were the guilty party. But, I agree, we need to be certain of his innocence. Let's hope your next interview will clear it up. I too have been reviewing this case and this is a copy of my draft report.'

He handed a sheet of A4 to Nick. He had spent quite some time on his investigations and was satisfied that he had come to some sensible and long-needed conclusions. It read

This is a report on my investigations of the loss of 100 Morphine tablets.

The tablets were on the trolley operated by Nurse Dawn Evernden. This was confirmed by the Nurse in charge of the Pharmacy on the recording sheet for the start of day. The only time that the trolley was left unattended was at Ward 7, when Nurse Evernden was called to assist

Dr Maitland with a patient who was in danger of falling out of bed. Neither Nurse Evernden nor Dr Maitland can recall anyone going near the trolley at that time, though they were involved with the patient and their attention was on him.

At the end of her shift, Nurse Evernden discovered the shortage and covered it up by taking a jar of pills from Nurse Susan Davies's trolley. The monthly audit was not done, an over-sight due to a large number of patients arriving from a coach crash and the pharmacy nurse was on holiday. Her deputy overlooked the audit in the rush for medication for the passengers of the coach.

Sadly, Nurse Davies was overcome to think that she might be accused of stealing the pills and she ended many years of faithful service by taking her own life. Our condolences have been forwarded to her husband and three children.

The police are now investigating the matter, and Detective Inspector Nicholas Price is conducting ongoing interviews.

The following observations, decisions and changes are the result of my enquiries.

1.1.1.   End of day recording of the trolley contents by the Pharmacy Nurse seems to have lapsed and will be restarted immediately.

1.1.2.   Every opportunity will be taken to keep the trolley lids closed during the day.

1.1.3.   The monthly audit will be scrapped and will be replaced by a bi-weekly audit.

1.1.4.   Nurse Evernden will return to work after a short period of re-training, to work on the wards. The tragic results of her actions could not have been foreseen and the cover-up was out of character. She will continue to be of interest in the police enquiries.

1.1.5.   Dr Maitland was in the ward at the time the trolley was vulnerable and he will continue to be of interest in the police enquiries.

Signed

M.J A Upton   CEO

Copies to the Board, DI Price(for information), Dr Maitland, Nurse Evernden, her Union Rep and the Pharmacy

When Nick finished reading, he placed the paper on the desk.. Dr Upton added 'You can see that our conclusions are almost identical, except for the treatment of Nurse Evernden, which is an internal matter anyway. That is very gratifying.'

He was sure that his efforts would be appreciated by the Board of the Trust, though they would not be happy that the stolen tablets would be out on the streets causing more misery.

As Nick was leaving, he paused at Helen's desk, a little unsure how to proceed. At least, Liz was out of the room. Helen looked up with her usual gleaming smile. 'Was there something else?' she asked. The detective was more used to asking questions, rather than answering them and hesitated before replying. ' Er...Would you like to meet for a drink after work?' There, he thought, that wasn't difficult, was it?

Helen flashed another smile. 'I'd like that a lot,' she said, 'Thank you for asking me.'

'The Cumberland. Five thirty?' he asked.

'I'll be there,' Helen said and went back to her typing as

Dr Upton came out of his office. Nick met Liz in the doorway as he left. It had been a long time since he had arranged a date and he had been worried that he would bungle the invitation. He walked with a lighter step down the long corridor, which suddenly seemed a lot shorter than it normally was.

NINETEEN

Alex Chisholm lived in a bungalow on the outskirts of the village. Surrounded by a neat garden, with short-clipped lawns, it was probably the smartest in the row of six, the colourful flower beds catching the eye of passers-by. As it stood on the route out of the village and up into the wooded hills beyond, many a walker stopped to admire and comment on the garden. Alex considered this a problem in the days when she was gardening, as the ensuing conversations held up the work. On the other hand, such pleasant interest from strangers was a bonus, so she didn't complain, even when a conversation made her late for her other interest – golf. David had often suggested that the only thing missing from her garden was a putting green and there were days when she thought it wouldn't be a bad idea, but it had never materialised.

And now it never would. She had got to the painful stage. Back pain was worst because it prevented her bending and weeding flower beds was all bending work, but it had to be done. Jim Parton had said weeks rather than months. Six weeks? Two weeks? She was definitely losing weight, comments about which she was managing to deflect by blaming golf and gardening and old age, but that wasn't going to work for ever, soon the cat would be out of the bag and everyone would know. She wasn't looking forward to the universal sympathy. She was the little toughie, remember? She wasn't particularly religious either, but there was something comforting with the thought that she would be with Anthony again.

She often thought of Anthony when she was gardening. He would have loved it here. They had planned so many

114

things, in fact, she still used the plan that he drew up while they were in Africa. The giant Chusan Palm in the front garden was a constant reminder of Africa and a matter of pride that it had thrived here – Anthony had said it would.

But now Anthony was not here and Alex relied on her memories, her family and her fellow-golfers for company. Jon and Maddy usually visited at least once a week, Jon more frequently than Maddy. They kept her up to date with what they were doing at school and in their lives in general, in fact, Alex felt that Jon spoke to her in preference to his parents. Perhaps her wider experience of the world added some weight to her advice when it was called for.

She was standing next to the palm, trowel in hand, ready to attack the weeds which had dared to take root in a flower bed, when the swish of tyres announced Jon's arrival, followed by Maddy, red-faced after a cycle race up the hill.

'OK. You win.' she said to her brother, who held his grandmother's gate open for his sister to pass through.

'You were doing all right until that dog ran out. Good job you didn't fall off, he'd have had you by the throat,' Jon replied with a grin.

'You might have waited for me, though,'

'Then I wouldn't have won,' Jon laughed. 'Better luck next time!'

The parked their cycles against the garage wall.

Alex put down her trowel. She wouldn't do much weeding now she had visitors. 'I bet you're both ready for some refreshment. Juice for two, is it?'

'Please!' they chorused and sat down on a bench in the sunniest spot in the garden.

Ice cubes rattled in the glasses of orange juice as Alex

put three drinks down on the table, then sat on one of the chairs to face her grandchildren.

'Well, what's new?' she asked.

'Not a lot,' Jon said, as a look passed between him and Maddy.

'What about you, Maddy? Anything happening? New boyfriend?'

'No, it's the same for me. Not a lot.' The look returned. Alex knew better than to push. There was obviously something they wanted to tell her. It would come out in time.

'Well, I have some news. I was going to sell my car. Getting too old to drive, you know. It's worth about five thousand pounds, so I've decided to give the car to Jon and five thousand pounds to Maddy to buy a car when she's old enough.'

There was a momentary silence as the news sank in. Jon's jaw dropped and Maddy pushed her hair back with both hands and held it there, almost afraid to move in case it was a dream from which she didn't want to wake up. Then both grandchildren spoke together in a babble.

'Are you sure?'

'Gran, that's wonderful!'

'Do you mean it?'

'But that's too much!'

'I've never...'

'I can't believe it.'

'I'm amazed!'

'Gran, you're too kind.'

'Wait till I tell Dad!'

They hugged their Gran. They hugged each other. Tears

of joy and disbelief rolled down Maddy's pretty cheeks, while Jon tried to hide his by blowing his nose.

When she could get a word in, Alex asked, 'How does that sound?' though the answer was obvious from her grandchildren's excited reaction.

'It sounds great,' Jon said, 'but how are you going to get to golf without a car?'

He didn't know that it wouldn't be a problem for long. She had probably played her last game of golf, though no-one else knew that at the moment.

'My playing partner, Sally, lives just down the road. We often travel together, so it's no problem.' That will keep up the pretence, she thought.

'I don't know how to thank you, Gran,' said Maddy. 'I've never seen so much money.'

' You don't have to. Now that's my news, how are the driving lessons going, Jon?'

'OK I suppose,' That look again.

'Gary's a good teacher, your Dad says.'

Jon looked down at his feet, avoiding eye contact.

'Yes, I suppose so.' followed by a glance to Maddy.

'When's your next lesson with him?'

'I... I...er....don't know.'

'What is it you're trying not to tell me?'

'Nothing!' they both said.

'We can't tell you.' Maddy blurted out.

'So there is something. Well, if you won't tell me I'll have to ask your Mum or Dad.'

'We don't know what to do,' Jon said with desperation in his voice. 'Dad said to keep it in the family.

Maddy joined in 'But you're family so I suppose...' she

looked at Jon, her face asking the obvious question. He nodded his approval.

'...I suppose we can tell you. But you mustn't let on that we've told you.'

'OK. You've got my word. So, tell me, Jon.'

'Well, Gran. It's like this. We've had a letter at home. An anonymous letter with 'To whom it may concern' in letters cut from a newspaper on the envelope. Inside was a letter which said that whoever it was sent to had done something that the family wouldn't like and that the sender knew about it and would be in touch with a demand for money. Blackmail. Was that about right, Maddy?'

She nodded.

Jon continued. 'We don't know which of us it's addressed to. It won't be Dad, he's a high-up doctor. It won't be Mum, she's so straightforward and honest. So it must be one of us.'

'So what have you two been doing to attract a blackmail letter?'

'Well, I thought it was great of Gary to offer driving lessons and I was enjoying driving, He took me to all sorts of places. But then one day we had to go to Liverpool and then Rhyl. The Mersey Tunnel was brilliant and we passed through lots of places in North Wales I'd never been to. We picked up a suitcase in Rhyl and we had to deliver it to a man at Bangor Races a couple of days later. He was the one who was stabbed at Bangor, you might have seen it on the news.'

She nodded and waited patiently for him to finish.

'It turned out that we were carrying drug money. Ten thousand pounds. I'm sure I'm the one the letter is intended for but I didn't know anything about the money. Honestly, Gran. Gary said my L-plates were useful as a kind of camouflage.'

'So have you still got the money?' she asked.

'No, Gary handed it to someone else who said he'd been sent to collect it, but we didn't think he had. I think he was the one who did the stabbing and now the wrong people have got the money.'

'That could be a problem,' Alex observed, then she asked 'What about you, Maddy? What do you think about this letter?'

'I thought it would be me.'

'Why? What have you done?'

'One evening, we were at Kelly's house.'

'We?'

'Kelly, Suzy and me. We were dressing up, playing music and Kelly produced a bottle of vodka. We didn't drink a lot. Didn't get drunk or anything. When Kelly was getting some of her mum's dresses for us to try on, I took my jumper and jeans off and I was singing and dancing around in my bra and pants. Suzy was filming me on her phone and I told her to delete the photos afterwards. I don't think she did, because she showed them to her boyfriend. I think they are going round school by now and I'm so worried. Mum and Dad would be very upset if they find out. And that's what the letter said - '...I know how your family will react when I tell them'. So I think it's directed at me.'

'It could be Suzy's boyfriend sending the letter. What's his name? Am I likely to know him?'

'It's Duncan. Duncan Baker. You know, Gary's son.'

Alex thought hard. She had promised not to say

119

anything to David and Chrissy and would keep that promise. She couldn't accuse Gary or Duncan face to face, they might be completely innocent. She might have a word with Gary if she came across him, though what she would say short of an out-and-out accusation would be a problem. The letter might not be for either Jon or Maddy; perhaps David or Chrissy may have something they'd prefer to be kept secret. Or it may be a hoax.

She felt tired and helpless, not a feeling she was used to; her sharp mind would have cut through to a solution, but her body was being taken over by the evil growing inside it and the weariness took over.

'I don't think we can do much at the moment,' she said. 'I suggest we wait and see if the follow-up ever arrives. It could be just a cruel hoax and you will have been worrying over nothing.'

They weren't entirely convinced, but agreed to wait and see.

'You're looking tired all of a sudden, Gran. You need a rest,' Maddy said.

'I am, Maddy. You're right. I think it's old age, you know. Golf and gardening don't mix and I've done both today. I think I'll go for a lie-down.'

'Good idea,' Jon put in 'and it's time we went. Thanks for the drinks, Gran. And the chat. I feel better now it's out in the open. Well, almost.'

Maddy took the empty glasses into the kitchen and washed them, then the youngsters collected their bikes from the garage wall and pedalled off down the hill. For her part, Alex went into the bungalow and crashed out on the settee. She really was tired.

TWENTY

Nick Price sat in the foyer of the Cumberland Arms watching through the glass doors for Helen's arrival. He was almost bubbling with anticipation. It had been a long time since he'd been out on a date – work, work and more work was the excuse he used, but secretly he felt too awkward to ask anyone to join him. The only women he met were policewomen and others he met in the course of his duties. Nothing wrong with policewomen, he thought, but he preferred a relationship with someone who was unconnected with work. He had dated a WPC once and felt as though he'd had a gruelling interview at the end of it. There had been no goodnight kiss, no exchange of phone numbers – they met regularly at work – and they went dutch on the drinks. She was clearly sizing up the competition for the next promotion. Never again.

When it came to the women he met in the course of his duties, they were already in trouble with one problem or another and he did not fancy picking up the pieces in broken lives, however sympathetic he felt. Dating for sympathy would be inappropriate, anyway, and could be seen as taking advantage.

But all his awkwardness and reticence had vanished when he met Helen Fletcher. Her beaming smile, those azure blue eyes, her welcoming approach as she sat behind her desk, were imprinted on his memory. 'Am I getting too sentimental?' he asked himself as phrases like 'a vision of loveliness' wafted through his mind. He recalled the husky voice saying 'Can I help you?' when he first visited Dr Upton. He could hear it now as he watched the door for

121

her arrival.

'Good evening, Nick.' The voice came from behind him. He turned, to find those eyes and the welcoming smile sitting behind him in her wheelchair.

'Helen, there you are!' was all he could manage.

'I came from the top car park. I can't manage those steps,' she said, indicating the long flight up to the front door.

'Of course not,' Nick said, 'but I didn't realise...' His hands flapped, loosely indicating the wheelchair.

'That's understandable. You've only seen me behind a desk and I don't use this in the office.'

'Well, now you're here, let's have a drink. The bar's this way. Do you prefer me to push or drive yourself?'

'I'll drive, if you don't mind. I've suffered from too many amateur pushers in the past.'

She smiled at him, and her classification of amateur pushers almost felt like a compliment to Nick.

They entered the bar and chose a corner table.

'What can I get you?' Nick asked.

'A Mediterranean Tonic, please. No ice.'

He returned from the bar with their drinks, having chosen a fresh orange with crushed ice for himself. They settled down with their drinks and caught up on events at the hospital, their only common ground. Helen reported that Dr Upton's recommendations had been accepted by the Board but there was no progress on who had taken the pills. Nick had nothing new to add to what Helen already knew of the investigations and conversation seemed likely to peter out.

'I suppose you're wondering how I ended up in the

wheelchair,' Helen said, injecting a new subject. 'Most people do.'

'I didn't like to ask,' Nick explained, 'but if you'd like to tell me I'll be happy to listen, unless it's too painful for you.'

'No, there are no painful memories. The short answer is that I fell off a horse.'

'Oh. I'd have thought that was painful. What's the long answer?' Nick wanted to know.

'Mummy says I could ride before I could walk. As a child, I always had a pony. We're a horsey family. Daddy has a couple of point-to-pointers and he plays polo. Mummy is District Commissioner for the Pony Club. We had good ponies as I grew up and I was in the club teams for show jumping, cross country and tetrathlon.'

'What's tetrathlon?' Nick asked, puzzled by the unfamiliar term.

'It's a competition in four disciplines, shooting, swimming, running and riding. It's a major recruiting ground for the Olympic modern pentathlon.'

'Serious stuff, then?'

'Oh yes. It's international as well. We have visiting teams from America, Australia, Canada and, of course, there are times when we went abroad.' She paused to sip her drink, then continued. 'I was on the short list for the London Olympics and we were in training...'

'Don't tell me you tackled one of those high fences,' Nick interrupted.

'No. I've come off horses and ponies all my life. Daddy used to say 'You can't call yourself a rider until you've fallen off a horse'. You learn to roll or fall as safely as you can. But that time I wasn't doing anything dangerous. Four of us were trotting along out in the hills. We were passing some dog walkers when one of the dogs, a terrier that sticks in my mind, ran out yapping and spooked my horse, which shied to one side and off I came. I landed awkwardly on a rock and it caused a small injury to my spinal cord, such that my legs are weak and I have difficulty walking, hence the wheelchair. On the bright side, I've learnt some new things.'

'Like what?'

'Wheelchair basketball. That's really enjoyable. I've joined a club which has its own sports chairs. Gets a little rough at times, but it's fun. And I help out at a disabled riding group from time to time.'

'So, you are busy in your spare time as well?'

'Yes. Sorry about the long answer but you did ask,' she smiled.

'I did. And it was very interesting. I've never met an Olympic athlete before.'

'I'm hardly that. I didn't make the team as a result of the injury.

'Well, I think you deserve a medal for what you've been through.'

'Thank you, Nick. That's enough about me. What about you? How has your life been?'

'Nowhere near as exciting as yours. Left school, went to university to read criminology and joined the police. I played a variety of sports – football, tennis, did a bit of skiing, swimming, of course. I learnt to dive on holiday in Egypt, that was fun. A totally different environment. I've had promotion since I joined the police, Detective Inspector now. Touch wood, I've never had any injuries, hence my ignorance of hospital procedures. Compared with your CV I've had a fairly humdrum life.'

'I wouldn't say that. I'm sure your life in the police can be very exciting at times. It's not all seeking out stolen pills, is it?'

'No, and it's not all hundred-mile-an-hour car chases either, but, I agree, it does have its moments.'

They discussed the possibility of a meal and settled for bar snacks which they enjoyed with another drink. Their other interests included theatre and films and it wasn't very long before they were arranging a cinema visit. They exchanged personal phone numbers and Nick, who had been so reticent about making a date in the first place, was surprised that another date had been made with such ease.

As they started to leave, Helen said, 'I like you, Nick, very much. I'm looking forward to our next date. You have passed the little test that I set for new friends. I feel comfortable with you because not once have you mentioned my wheelchair or my disability being a snag. I like that.'

He walked with her to her car and helped to stow her wheelchair in the boot. Then he leaned in as she sat in the driver's seat and kissed her lightly. 'Good night, and thanks for a great evening.' 'Thank you,' she responded, 'I've enjoyed it too,' and took his lapel to pull him down. They repeated the kiss, but this time, not so lightly.

'Thanks again. I'll see you soon.' Nick was reluctant to let her go as she started the engine and looked up at him. That beaming smile again as she wound up the window 'Good night' they both said as she drove slowly away.

Nick watched her tail-lights vanish through the gate. His

hospital visits would be more frequent from now on.

TWENTY ONE

David Maitland was deep in thought. He had more or less gone into his shell, so deep were his thoughts. He knew that his reputation was sound, he was well-respected in the village, in the hospital and in the profession. His advice was sought not just by the staff at St Agnes'; he received many requests for advice and assistance from doctors at other hospitals in the region. The fact that he was of interest to the police was devastating. The fact that such news would fly round to all and sundry was even more so.

The nature of the crimes was also so far out of character that nobody who knew him would have believed that he would even be considered as a suspect. Yet there it was. He was present when the drugs went missing. He was alone with his father at the end. In a way, he really couldn't blame the police for being suspicious, for putting two and two together. But was he the only one to think they had added it up to five?

At least he hadn't been arrested and charged. The search of his office was undignified. The search of his home was entirely uncalled for. Chrissy was mortified. He had protected her and the kids from all sorts of problems in their everyday lives, but he couldn't protect them from the shame of having policemen searching their home. The police had asked him what he had done with the unused tablets – there were a hundred in the jar. How can I answer that apart from a straight denial? They came back with 'But you would say that.' To say he wouldn't have a clue how to dispose of them illegally would have brought a similar response. So, if he hadn't disposed of them, they must still be here, and the search went on.

Then there was that letter. 'To whom it may concern', indeed. It could only be directed at him. Coming on top of all this police interest it could only have come from someone who knew him quite well. Someone who had a grudge. He racked his brains to think of who that might be. All his promotions had been on merit. He hadn't climbed over anyone to get to the top of his profession. He could think of no-one who disliked him, certainly not enough to resort to blackmail. He hadn't had a disagreement with anyone – there was that little spat with Gary but they had got over it. We're old friends, he comes to the house, Uncle Gary, teaching Jon to drive, can't be him.

On the other hand, it could be jealousy. I've made the most of my chances, Gary hasn't, with the result of the difference in our lifestyles. Of course, I have a better salary, but I've worked for it, he must realise that. But then, anyone can be a suspect. I'm one, aren't I, even though I know I'm innocent? Anyone can be, but I think I'm clutching at straws to think that Gary is the blackmailer.

He went through the letter in his mind. The words were branded on his brain as though he had memorised it as Maddy memorises her acting parts. You know how you did wrong. I've done nothing wrong that I know of. Others, including the police, think I have, but I haven't. I know how your family will react when I tell them So is it something other than the current enquiries that I am supposed to have done?

One final thought struck him. If I am so innocent, is the letter intended for someone else in the family? Chrissy?

The kids? Oh God! It gets worse!

Chrissy found herself staring at a kitchen shelf. Not just any shelf, but the one where the letter rack stood, containing bills to be paid, reminders, theatre tickets and that letter. It was transfixed in her mind ever since it arrived.

Eighteen years of worry bubbled up inside her. Always at the back of her mind, it now took centre stage. How was she to tell David that his first-born son might be Gary's? How was she to tell Jon that Uncle Gary was, in fact, his father? What would happen to what had been, for the most part, a happy marriage?

Many a time she had relived that morning when she woke up to find herself naked in bed and that awful prospect had forced itself into her mind. A hazy memory of walking to the bottom of the staircase with Gary's arm around her waist. She had felt safe, though she had fallen once and Gary had picked her up. His arm had tightened around her as she sighted the ordeal of the long staircase and - nothing. Complete oblivion until she awoke next morning. From then on, preparations for the wedding were a blur. The over-riding thoughts in her mind were of that night, a constant question for almost eighteen years. Until this.

She was sure the writer of that heinous letter was Gary. No-one else knew, except Linda and Aanya, and they would have kept her secret, she knew. Why was he doing this? She doubted that he was short of money to the extent of blackmail, though she had no special knowledge of his finances, except to say that Sheryl had a job to keep them

129

afloat each month.

She looked around her kitchen. The envy of their visitors, it contained all the labour-saving devices. An induction hob on the French cooker with a control panel which looked as though it was designed by NASA; an American fridge freezer that kept Jon and Maddy supplied with cold drinks in the summer; the homely central island-cum-breakfast bar where plans for the day were made. She was about to shatter all of this when the news came out, as the letter promised it would.

But Gary hadn't said anything before, so why bring it up now? Part of her took a little hope from the thought that perhaps she was not the target. But who else could be? She knew about David's problems at the hospital, but that was common knowledge, especially after the police had searched her house and therefore it was not a matter for blackmail. Jon hasn't done anything out of the ordinary, just driving lessons with Gary. He was at Bangor Races with Gary when that man was murdered but he was on the way home when they heard about that. And Maddy? She had spent her days with Kelly and Suzy, sometimes at our house, sometimes at Kelly's. We would have noticed if she was involved with drugs or booze. Just happy teenagers.

So perhaps it is aimed at me after all!

Maddy and Jon sat on a bridge over the brook that ran through the village.

'Remember playing Pooh-sticks here?' he asked, as he selected another pebble out of his hand and aimed at a floating leaf.

'Yes. Amazing what amuses you when you're little.'

130

'And now we're involved in blackmail. Not much fun being grown-up, is it?

'No. But who do you think sent it?'

'I don't know. At first, I thought it was for me and Gary had sent it, but that can't be true.'

'Why not?'

'Well, I could blackmail him for the same reason, carrying drug money. Perhaps it was Duncan or even Suzy, if they had found out what Gary and I were doing. Those two might have done something like this for fun without thinking about the effect on the rest of the family.'

'That's true. They could be including me over those photos. I know Mum and Dad would be disappointed about me on Facebook in my undies, but it's not the end of the world if they found out.'

'As Gran says, it might turn out to be a hoax, or fizzle out on its own. Let's wait and see.'

He sank two more leaves before they mounted their bikes and rode slowly home.

TWENTY TWO

Gary had waited until they were walking home. He had made his regular visit to the Ram's Head to accompany Sheryl and had sat mulling over a pint as he waited for her to clear up, trying to decide whether to unburden himself to her there or leave it until later. He knew there would be an almighty row that he had kept it quiet all this time. It wasn't just Vince's ten grand that he owed. Domestic bills and his debt to Barry Meadows would also be included in his confession. He knew this would be one confession that would not receive absolution. He wasn't that sure how to begin. He knew the local debts were all his own silly fault; Vince's money was a different matter altogether. He would have to explain how it arose; that he'd been collecting drug money; that Vince could be vicious if crossed; that a man had already been murdered. It was a different world from what Sheryl was used to. Would she understand? Would she support him through this? Perhaps she would after she had cooled down, if she cooled down. He had been in debt before but not to this extent, and she had helped him through it, but this was different. Could this be the end of their partnership?

Sheryl locked the pub door, shook it to make sure that it was locked, dropped the keys into her handbag and released her blonde hair which had been confined in a pony-tail to comply with the regulations. As she swung her head from side to side to shake it out, Gary caught the aroma of her perfume. She linked arms with Gary to start the walk home. It was a warm evening and she was enjoying the freedom after a busy night at work, the breeze on her face, even the moths and the flying beetles clanging against the globes of the street lamps. She was at peace with the world.

'You're quiet tonight,' she commented. 'Problems at work?'

'Sort of.' He was evasive, but he knew he had to spoil this calm evening with his confessions. He could see from her expression that she expected more than 'Sort of.' He needed to amplify it.

'There's been an investigation at work. Some pills went missing and we've all been questioned – a couple of nurses, David and me. Poor old Sue Davies committed suicide as a result, so it's quite serious. And now the police are involved.'

'Well, they surely don't suspect the doctors? I mean, you and David have been there for years.'

'The problem is, I took them. But nobody knows yet.'

'Why on earth would you take them? What were they? Viagra or something?'

'I made a silly remark, like I usually do, just a bit of banter, to one of the patients, a chap from Liverpool, Vince his name was, and he didn't like it. I think he was looking for an opportunity to steal some morphine tablets. Turns out he was a drug dealer and threatened me with reporting me to the Board if I didn't steal some for him. But that wasn't enough, because he then wanted me to collect some of his drug money from Rhyl.'

Sheryl was putting two and two together.

'So is that why you went to Liverpool and Rhyl with Jon the other week?'

Gary took a deep breath.

'Actually, it was. Yes.'

Sheryl stopped walking and turned Gary to face her.

'Have you lost your mind?

He looked away, unable to meet her steely gaze.

'Is there anything else I need to know? If so, tell me now.'

'Well, we had about ten grand sitting in the car all weekend until I could take it to Bangor Races to hand it over on the following Tuesday.'

'So, you've got rid of it? At least that's something.'

They walked on in silence while Sheryl considered this new revelation.

'Why do I feel there's more to come?'

'Because the guy, Terry, that I was supposed to give it to was knifed in the toilets before the handover. I was waiting by the gate, as arranged and two guys rolled up and said Terry had been delayed and they'd been asked to collect it.'

'So you gave it to them?'

'Yes.'

'So we're rid of it?'

'Sort of "

'It gets worse, doesn't it?'

'Yes. They were from a rival outfit, so Vince has lost his money. He's blaming me and says I've got to pay it back to him. He's threatening me because he wants his money back and by all accounts, he can be vicious. Honestly, Sheryl, I don't know what to do.'

'There's only one thing you can do. You'll have to go to the police and have him put away.'

'But I can't do that. To do that I'd have to admit to stealing the pills and I'll be struck off. We'll be ruined. No money. No job.'

She was in a quandary as to her next move. A stand–up row on the roadside wouldn't help, though she felt like handing out some violence herself. Solutions were hard to find.

'You need to get him off your back. You'll have to get a loan and pay him off. You're on a good salary, so paying it off won't be a problem.'

'It's not so easy, Sheryl. I owe so much money, a lender will be hard to find.'

'You owe so much money?' She repeated his words unbelievingly. 'What else do you owe money for?'

'The domestic bills for a start. Then there's three phones, yours, mine and Duncan's. I haven't paid anything for two months. And there's Barry Meadows.'

'The bookie. So that's where all the money goes.'

'Well, when I got behind with the bills, I only needed one big winner to put me straight.'

'So how much do you owe the bookie?'

'He reckons it's about a thousand.'

'Gary, you've been a bloody fool. It's going to take ages to clear all this. We'll have to have a different arrangement for paying bills.'

She was calm and business-like now but Gary knew the storm would arrive when they were home and indoors. He'd seen Sheryl's temper in action at the pub, giving an errant customer the sharp edge of her tongue. He had better try to put a positive spin on the situation before they reached home. She might not like it, but it might work.

'There is one thing I've done to raise some money...'

But he never finished his sentence. Suddenly, they were bathed in headlights and a car engine roared as it accelerated down the pavement behind them.

Sheryl turned, screamed and made an unsuccessful attempt to pull Gary out of its path. The car struck Gary and he flew across the pavement, knocking Sheryl over in the process. His head hit the cast iron railings and his lifeless body dropped to the ground. The car continued on its way, but Sheryl was unable to take the number in the confusion. She had the merest glimpse of the driver as she and Gary fell in a tangled heap.

TWENTY THREE

Chief Inspector Tom Cameron of Cheshire Constabulary rang his inspector at 11.30 that night.

'Evening, Nick. Sorry about this, but you'll need to get down to Thornhill. There's been a hit-and-run fatality. Soon as you can.'

When Nick arrived at the road between the Ram's Head and the Cumberland Arms, blue ambulance lights illuminated a small crowd, silent in respect for the huddled shape lying against the cast iron fence. The ambulance crew confirmed that there was no sign of life despite their efforts at resuscitation. The gentleman's partner was being cared for in the ambulance. They gave the victim's name as Gary Baker, a doctor who they knew by sight from Thornhill Park Hospital. This had been confirmed by his partner, Miss Sheryl Manton, manager of the Ram's Head Inn, now in the ambulance. Nick made a note of this information as it was given to him by the paramedic. He had phoned the station to arrange tapes and floodlights when he was on the way down. It may have been a road accident or we may be looking at a crime scene, he explained to the night staff. Better to be covered right from the start. He took a look at Gary's crumpled body with his head against the railings and a large pool of blood beneath it on the paving stones. Better get Forensics to see it in situ before we take it to the morgue, he thought, and got a constable to set it in motion while he went into the ambulance to see Miss Manton. His initial questions would need to be gently put.

'Hello, Miss Manton, I'm Detective Inspector Nick Price. I'm very sorry about your loss. Are you up to

137

answering a few questions now so we can get to work finding out who did this?' Sheryl had passed through the stage of floods of tears. Gone was the confident, outgoing manager of the local pub; in her place, Nick saw a beaten grey shell of a woman, grey faced with lank blonde hair. Her tears had washed the remains of the day's make-up from her face as she sat, slumped, staring at the floor of the ambulance, her refuge from the disaster outside. She nodded. 'I'll do my best. What do you want to know?'

'To start with, could you tell me what you remember of what happened?'

'Gary and I were walking home after I finished work, like he always did, and suddenly a car mounted the pavement behind us. It knocked Gary into me. We both fell and he hit his head on the railings. The car didn't stop. Just carried on.'

'Were you injured at all?'

'I went down on my left elbow. It still hurts but the paramedic says I'll be ok, just bruised. And I scuffed my knee on the pavement and my hip is sore where I fell. I've had a once over from the crew and they say I'm lucky it's no worse.'

'Well, that's good. Now, did you recognise the car?'

'Not really. It happened so quick. Gary and I tumbled together; all I saw as it passed was a blaze of lights. It was gone before I could see the number plate. I seem to recall a glimpse of the driver. He had grey hair, but that's all I remember.'

'We'll need to work out if this was accidental or a deliberate attack. Is there anyone who might have done this deliberately?'

'No-one that I can think of immediately. But Gary and I were talking just before the car...er...you know.' She couldn't bring herself to mention what the car had done. The tears started again at the thought. 'I need to sort it out in my own mind.'

Nick could see that she was so badly shaken that he would get nowhere tonight. 'Could I call to see you tomorrow morning? It will give you time to think,' he asked.

'Yes please. Thank you.'

Nick showed her out to the police car and wished her goodnight as she left.

He then joined the forensic crew who were examining the body.

'Not much to tell,' the doctor said, 'It looks as though it was the head injury that killed him, though he's taken a terrific blow to his legs and hip, where the car struck him. I've taken all the photographs I need so you can take him to the morgue now and I'll have a look at him in the morning.'

Duncan and Suzy were at the door to meet Sheryl. A car drawing up at this time of night had brought them off the settee and up to the window as they watched television. When they saw it was a police car they ran to the door. 'What's up, Mum?' Duncan asked, 'Where's Dad?'

'He's not coming back, son, He's...he's...had an accident,' She couldn't face the reality of admitting that Gary was dead.

'Is he alright? Has he gone to hospital?' Questions came thick and fast as Sheryl came in, hung up her coat and burst into tears. She sank into the settee.

'I'm sorry to tell you but...he's dead, Duncan. A car ran

into him and killed him.'

'You mean – dead? He's not coming back? Ever?' Duncan and Suzy sat either side of Sheryl and each held a hand.

'It was awful,' Sheryl went on. 'We were just walking home, just before the Cumberland, and a car shot from behind us and hit him. We both fell in a heap and Dad hit his head on the railings. Somebody was just leaving the Cumberland and rang 999. The ambulance was there in no time as it's so close to Aggies but there was nothing they could do. The police came and took over. They'll be coming for a statement tomorrow morning. By the way, where's our car? Dad usually leaves it on the drive. Have you been out in it?'

Duncan ran to the door and looked out.

'You're right. It's not there. Somebody must have taken it.'

'But you've been here all evening. You would have heard it. Doors shutting. Engine starting.'

'We didn't hear anything, did we Suzy? We had loud music on.' Which may have been true, though the guilty look which passed between them suggested that more was going on than they were prepared to admit.

'Can I make you a cup of tea, or would you like something stronger? Suzy asked.

'Tea will be fine, thanks,' Sheryl tried to smile for the girl's benefit. It was a friendly, comforting thought; Suzy was like that.

'And then can Duncan walk me home? Doctor Baker usually does it when we're late.'

'Yes, of course.' Suzy's use of the present tense was a

reminder that Gary was not there. It prompted more tears from Sheryl.

There was a long night ahead of her...

TWENTY FOUR

Nick Price arrived at the Baker house at a reasonable hour next morning, allowing time for Sheryl to come to terms with her new situation and to get over the trauma of the previous night. She was already up and about and looked more like her normal self, apart from the puffiness around her eyes, which make-up had failed to disguise. Other than that, her blonde hair was back in place and her demeanour had changed from the shell of a woman that was slumped in the ambulance to her normal business-like self. She wore a white blouse and black trousers which showed off her voluptuous figure while remaining respectful to Gary's passing. She would be behind the bar again this morning, if only to delegate duties to cover her absence as a result of her bereavement. She opened the door for Nick before he had got out of his car and greeted him with an apology for how she had been the previous night.

'No need for an apology,' Nick said, 'I hope you had some sleep after all that had happened?'

'I managed a few hours,' she replied 'Now, I was making a pot of tea. Would you like one while we talk?'

'Yes, please. Milk, no sugar in mine.'

She ushered him into the lounge and vanished into the kitchen to make the tea. Nick found himself in a pleasant room. It was clean and tidy, obviously a no-smoking family. A picture window looked out on to well-kept lawns and flower beds while inside were tasteful ornaments – not too many – on a green Westmoreland slate mantelpiece. An alcove to the right of the fireplace had been given over to

Gary's framed diplomas and degrees. A book-case contained a variety of books which gave a clue to the lifestyle of the family. Prominent were a couple on betting systems and a few autobiographies of top jockeys - obviously Gary's choice. Sheryl's interest lay in romantic novels but Nick was surprised to see some serious historical non-fiction amongst them. Then there were the classics, Dickens, Shakespeare, and poetry anthologies, plus a couple of encyclopaedias that had been made redundant by Wikipedia and the march of time.

'I take it mugs will be OK?' she asked, bringing in the teas. Nick nodded his approval.

'Mugs are fine,' he confirmed, then, as Sheryl sat on an armchair opposite to Nick on the settee, he asked her if she would go through the evening's events again. She did, neither adding nor omitting anything she had said previously.

Nick went on 'For our part, we have looked again at the scene with the benefit of daylight. We can see that the car mounted the pavement a long way back from the point of impact, far enough for even a drunk driver to have changed course to avoid an accident, and you said that the headlights were full on, so we can be fairly sure that the driver was fully aware of your presence ahead of him and this was deliberate. So, can you think of anyone who is likely to have wanted him dead?'

Sheryl shook her head. 'No, no..' she was on the verge of tears again and Nick decided to change tack.

'You all right, Mum?' Duncan had come into the room and was concerned to see his mother distressed.

She pulled herself together, 'Yes, Dunc. I'll be fine.

There's tea in the pot, you'll have to help yourself. You can bring it in here if you like.' She turned to Nick 'My son, Duncan,' she explained.

Nick continued. 'You'll be pleased to know we found your car. Abandoned in Green Shoots Garden Centre car park, just three hundred yards away. There's some damage to the nearside wing, the wing mirror is broken on that side and the broken glass matches some pieces we found at the scene, so we're pretty sure that your car was used. Just out of interest, why didn't he pick you up in the car instead of walking you home?'

'He always had a drink at the pub when he picked me up, so he wouldn't drink and drive. He was a doctor and had seen the results of that too often to take any risks.'

'Very sensible. That makes sense. Let's think about the car. Does Duncan drive it at all?'

'No. I haven't got a licence.' Duncan was quick to reply.

'Well, Doctor Baker's keys were amongst his belongings at the station; do you have keys, Miss Manton?'

'Yes, but I hardly ever drive the car. They're here, in my bag.' She rummaged in her handbag and brought them out to show him.

'Does anyone else have a key?'

'Well, he's...was giving my mate Jonathan driving lessons. Perhaps he has a key.' Duncan put in.

'And where will I find this Jonathan? I'll need to talk to him.'

'I'll give you his address. He's Jonathan Maitland.' Duncan took out his mobile and searched for Jon's address, which he wrote on a piece of paper and gave to Nick.

'Maitland? Is he related to Doctor Maitland at the

hospital?'

'Father and son,' Duncan said.

Nick was making mental connections.

'Did Doctor Baker get on well with Doctor Maitland?' he asked.

'Yes, as far as I know,' Sheryl replied. 'They were at Medical School together. Gary was an honorary uncle to their kids. Friends for years.'

'Well, we'll be needing fingerprints from you both and Jonathan, for elimination purposes. We'll catch up with you later in the day, perhaps. Can we go back to last night? Was there anyone who Doctor Baker had trouble with in any way?' Nick was staying away from words like 'enemies' which he felt applied in the underworld, not in a rural hospital environment.

Sheryl said, 'We had money problems. Doesn't everybody? But Gary had been a gambler for years and it was always a struggle keeping us afloat. He had dreams of the big winner which would solve all our problems, but it never happened. He said he owed money all over the place. It seems that some of these people were closing in on him. He owed Barry Meadows, the bookie, a thousand pounds and Meadows had wanted it paid off by the weekend. Then he mentioned someone called Vince from Liverpool. He owed him ten thousand pounds. Apparently, he had collected the money from Rhyl and was supposed to give it to someone else at Bangor Races, but he gave it to the wrong person. The man who was knifed at Bangor was something to do with it. I'm sorry, I've spent the night trying to sort it out in my own mind. Oh, Gary was blackmailed into stealing some pills at the hospital. I think

145

Vince was involved in that. I'm not exactly sure where they fitted into the story.'

Nick didn't press her further. He could ask her to go over it again when she had more time to think. Now he'd got a mammoth task. Contact North Wales Police about the Bangor killing. Contact Merseyside Police about Vince. Who was Vince and why did he need Gary to collect ten grand from Rhyl? Why Rhyl? The rest of the morning on the phone was in prospect. He prepared to leave.

'I'm sure you have questions you would like to ask. As regards what will happen next, I've asked WPC Jane Wycherley, our Community Welfare Officer, to come round this morning and put you in the picture.

'Just one thought.' Duncan had been thinking. 'They have CCTV at Green Shoots, don't they? Have you looked at that?'

'Good thought, Duncan. We looked at it earlier and whoever was driving the car knew exactly where the blind spots are. The lights came into the car park at the time we would expect them, but the bushes they have on some of the islands obscured the cars, both yours and the perpetrator's own car, which was driven off immediately afterwards. Of course, out here in the country, there are no other roadside businesses with CCTV to help us. End of the trail, I'm afraid.'

As Nick finished his explanation, a knock on the door heralded the arrival of Jane Wycherley, who Nick introduced and then discreetly left. Jane was the ideal person to take over now; practical, knowledgeable, sympathetic, she would look after Sheryl and Duncan through this dark period in their lives.

146

TWENTY FIVE

Nick tapped on his superior's door and entered when invited. Chief Inspector Tom Cameron was not known for his energy. His style was to let his staff do the leg work while he applied the brains of the team back in the office. It was his brains that were called for this morning.

'What have you got for me today, Nick? Hit and run was straight forward, was it?'

'Not really, boss,' Nick replied, and went through all the details he had picked up from Sheryl. At the end, he listed the phone calls he'd have to make to neighbouring forces, visits to the hospital and to the Maitland home and examination of the car which had been brought in from the car park on a low loader.

'It certainly isn't straightforward, but you seem to be on the right track so I'll leave you to it. Keep me informed, though. In case the Super takes an interest.'

Nick was happy to be allowed full rein on these cases. It would look good on his record and surely the Super had noticed how little Cameron did and how much Nick himself had been involved. Or was Cameron letting him loose hoping for him to fall down on a case? He was never sure how to read the situation. He usually had this thought on occasions such as last night, when he had received that phone call at 11.30pm.

He returned to his office and dialled his opposite number in North Wales Police. DI Dave Tudor, answered on two rings.

'Morning, Dave. Nick Price. Long time since we spoke.'

'Hi, Nick. How's things with you?

'So-so. Are you still investigating that knifing at Bangor?'

'Yes. And getting nowhere.'

'Well, last night we had a fatal hit and run and the guy's partner said that he was somehow involved in your murder. It's early days yet, but I thought I'd let you know. I do have a post code that you could check out for me. I'll email it to you. This case looks complicated but I'll contact you again when I have more information.'

"That'll be useful, Nick. Our victim was from Liverpool so we're in touch with Merseyside on this. Any help from you will be useful.'

'Who is your contact at Merseyside? I may need to contact them. As well.'

'DI is Diane Coleman.

'OK. I know Diane. Thanks. I'll be in touch. Bye.'

They both clicked off.

A uniformed constable knocked on Nick's door and came in carrying two small plastic evidence bags, each containing a piece of paper.

'Fingerprints has finished with the car now, Sir. He found these in the door pocket on the passenger side and thought you ought to see them straight away.' He put the bags on the desk.

'Thanks. I'm glad they're in bags; that fingerprint powder gets everywhere.'

The constable left and Nick examined the bags. Each contained a piece of paper on which was written a post code – one in Liverpool and one in North Wales. 'Where's LL18?' he thought. Which Brain of Britain decided to give the whole of North Wales the same post code? A quick Google check told him that LL18 was Rhyl. Liverpool and Rhyl. Sheryl mentioned those when they spoke. And the Bangor victim had a Liverpool connection. The dots are beginning to join up. Or are they?

He decided to ring Diane Coleman. This was like old times. As Nick was based in north-east Cheshire, close to the Welsh border and the south east corner of the Merseyside area, there had been many cases over the years where co-operation between forces was necessary to produce a solution. Improvements in the road system made it easier for the baddies to commit a robbery even as far south as Shropshire and make a swift getaway to the North West before the alarm was raised. No longer was the bobby on a bike a deterrent. Helicopters and high-speed cars and motorbikes were the order of the day. But it still took a human brain, or a collection of brains with local knowledge to stay ahead of the criminals and the co-operation between forces was crucial in this. As a result, he knew Dave Tudor and Diane Coleman very well indeed.

Diane answered with a brief 'C.I.D. DI Coleman.'

'Hi Diane. It's Nick Price.'

'How are the green fields today?' Diane asked.

'Fine, thanks. How's the concrete jungle?'

Banter over, they got down to business.

'We've had a fatal hit-and-run here and I think there are some connections with a case of yours. To complicate things, there are connections with a case Dave has in North Wales as well.'

'Ah, that'll be the murder at Bangor Races, then.'

'Correct. I haven't really got started on this one yet, but

I thought I'd let you know so that if anything comes up you'll keep me informed. A couple of things I know so far. I have a post code and a name, Vince. No surname, unfortunately. I'll put it on an email. I have some interviews to do now, so I'll be in touch soon.'

Nick finished the call and checked the next number. St Agnes' Hospital was to be his first port of call.

TWENTY SIX

'Hello. Doctor Upton's office. Helen speaking. How can I help you?'

Nick was thrilled to hear that husky voice again.

'Good morning, Helen. It's Nick. DI Price'

'There's no need for embellishments,' she laughed, ' I recognised your voice. How are you?'

'Fine, thanks. And you?'

'The same. So, to what do I owe the honour of this call?'

'It's business, I'm afraid. I need to see Doctor Upton. You've heard about Doctor Baker, I suppose?'

'Yes, his partner phoned in first thing this morning. It's so tragic. He was such a nice man. Was it an accident or shouldn't I ask?

'We don't know yet. There's a lot of work to do before we do. Of course, the bonus is that I'll get to see you again.' He was finding it difficult to keep to business. The couple of days since their date had seemed interminable and he was glad of the opportunity to see Helen again. She checked Doctor Upton's diary.

'He'll be free at 11.45 for 15 minutes. How does that suit you?

'Sounds fine. I'm hoping that your lunch break is 12 till 1?'

'Yes, it is.'

'Then I can take you to lunch. Hospital restaurant OK?'

'Sounds great. See you at 11.45 then.'

They hung up and Helen set about swapping lunch times with her assistant, Liz, who normally went at 12 o'clock. That little white lie was all in a good cause, she thought.

Doctor David Maitland would be free for a short chat at 11am. 'That's all I need,' Nick had said as he entered it in his diary. The morning was panning out pretty well. It was better to be fitted into the doctor's schedule like this rather than waving his warrant card and jumping the queue of patients who, let's face it, needed the doctor more than he did.

Promptly at 11am, Doctor Maitland's secretary showed him into the doctor's office,

'Good morning, Doctor Maitland. Thanks for seeing me at short notice. I'll be brief.

You will have heard the sad news about Doctor Baker, I assume?'

David nodded. 'Yes. It's very sad.'

Nick continued 'The only good thing to come out of his death is that he told his partner that he stole the pills that we have been so busy investigating. I'm sure you'll be relieved to know that we'll be closing that enquiry, though we'll continue to try to find where they went.

David visibly relaxed at the news. He hadn't been sure why the detective wanted to see him and had convinced himself that any news would be bad.

'That's a relief,' he said. 'You don't realise the pressure it puts on the family to be accused, a suspect, with home and office searched, all the time knowing that I was innocent.'

'I do understand,' Nick replied, 'And that pressure might just make a guilty person crack under the strain. Of course, at that stage I didn't know who was guilty and who was innocent.'

David was grudging with his reply. 'I suppose so. I'm glad it's over.'

'One other thing. Is your son, Jonathan, at home this afternoon?'

'I can ring him to make sure he is, but why do you need to see him?'

'We need to take his fingerprints...'

'What? Surely he's not a suspect?'

Nick avoided answering.

'I believe Doctor Baker was giving him driving lessons.'

David nodded. Nick went on.

'Doctor Baker's car was used in the hit-and-run, so we'll need your son's prints for elimination purposes.'

'Of course. I'll ring him straight away.

Thank you, Doctor Maitland. Life can return to normal now.'

He hoped it would as he left and made his way to a waiting area. He took his place among the patients, some of whom were anything but patient and vocally so; he hoped for a quiet moment to bring his notes up to date, whiling the time away for the next half-hour.

Just before 11.45 he presented himself at Helen's office and she confirmed that her boss was free and ready to meet Nick. She announced him and he tapped the door and entered.

'Good morning, Doctor Upton. Thank you for seeing me so promptly.'

'Good morning, DI Price. I understood there was some urgency, so here we are.'

'Yes. I'm assuming you have heard the news about

Doctor Baker.' Upton nodded. Nick continued ' I have to tell you that just before the incident he told his partner that he was responsible for taking the pills from Nurse Evernden's trolley,'

'You do surprise me,' Michael Upton said.

'Apparently it was as a result of blackmail by a patient. I've seen Doctor Maitland this morning to tell him this and that he is no longer under suspicion as far as we are concerned. No doubt you will be confirming the same from the hospital's point of view.'

'I will,' Doctor Upton replied. 'I will also have to see Nurse Evernden to explain the situation. It was fairly clear that she had not taken the pills, but she felt very guilty about the fact that they had been taken from her trolley; her suspension was as a result of her subterfuge with the late Nurse Davies's trolley. I will also, obviously, have to keep the Board informed as to these developments. As regards Doctor Baker, is there any information as to how this unfortunate event took place? Was it just an accident?'

'We are still looking into it, but first signs indicate that it was not an accident. That gives us a much more difficult problem to solve. Who would want to kill him? What starts as a simple case often turns out to be something more complicated. I suppose you have no idea of anyone within the hospital staff who might have had some kind of grudge against him?'

The administrator shook his head. 'Gary Baker was well thought of. He had been here for years and was popular with patients. One hears rumours about his forward, even suggestive, way with patients but no one has ever made an official complaint about him. So no, I cannot think of anyone who would have carried this out It would have to be a serious grudge to go to these lengths.'

Nick agreed and thought this was going to be one of those cases which built up its complications as it went along, and with nothing to go on at the start he just knew that he was in for a rough ride.

Michael Upton glanced at his watch and Nick realised his time was up, so he expressed his thanks for the administrator's time and left.

He found Helen waiting at the outer door into the corridor. He looked around for her wheelchair but there was no sign of it. Helen smiled at his confusion.

'If you're looking for my wheelchair, I'm not using it. The physio says I must walk more, and with you to support me, I can make it to the restaurant and back.' She linked arms and they made slow progress down the corridor.

At the restaurant, Helen was glad to find a chair. She sat down gratefully and Nick asked what she would like for lunch. She ordered a Prawn Sandwich and a glass of Orange Juice – the chewy one with the bits in, she stipulated. Nick went for a Ham and Cheese Sandwich and Apple Juice.

As they settled into their meal, she asked what had brought him to the hospital that morning. 'You asked on the phone whether we knew about Doctor Baker. Was there more to add?

'Not particularly. I met Doctor Maitland and told him he was off the hook and I needed to keep your boss up to date with developments., This will come out soon enough so keep it under your hat for now, but,' He leaned in towards her and whispered. 'Doctor Baker was the one who

155

took the pills from Nurse Evernden's trolley.'

'That's a surprise,' she said, 'I wouldn't have said he was the type to take drugs, especially considering where he works.'

'He wasn't taking them, he was blackmailed into it by a drug dealer.'

'That's very sad,' she said and lapsed into quiet thought. She had come to know Gary over the years and she felt real sorrow at his death.

Nick's hand slipped across the table and took hers gently. 'I'm sorry,' he said. 'I'm sure you will all miss him at the hospital.' He took comfort from the fact that she didn't withdraw from his touch.

With the subject changed, they chatted on, still comparing their past histories, family details, getting to know their likes and dislikes, all the things that go to making a firm foundation for a trusting relationship.

At ten to one they pushed their chairs back and made to return Helen to her office. Nick commented that it was fortunate that his appointment with Dr Upton coincided with Helen's lunch hour. They met a nurse in the doorway. She smiled at Helen. 'Early lunch today, Helen?' she asked.

'Something like that,' Helen made an off-hand remark and linked arms with Nick as they went into the corridor.

'But I thought you said....' he began.

Helen blushed and said 'I'm entitled to one little white lie, aren't I?'

Nick put on a comic imitation of a music hall policeman. 'It's an offence to tell lies to a hofficer of the law. I'll have to take you into custody,' he said.

'Yes, please,' was her reply.

156

At 2pm, Nick arrived at the Maitland house. Chrissy met him at the door, forewarned of his arrival. Her greeting was bland, neither gushing nor frosty; she didn't seem at all pleased to see him, although her husband had given her the good news about the missing pills – she was still stinging over last week's search of her home.

'Good afternoon, Mrs Maitland. Another officer will be along to take your son's fingerprints shortly, but perhaps I could have a word with him now. I'm still trying to piece together the background in this case.'

'Come in,' Chrissy said. 'I suppose you must.'

'Well, if we are to find out who killed Doctor Baker, I do need to make enquiries. Even if the incident was accidental, it could be a serious offence, such as causing death by dangerous driving, perhaps driving under the influence – of drugs or alcohol, failing to report an accident, so it's not all plain sailing, you see. I need all the information I can get, however irrelevant it seems at the time.'

'I suppose so,' she said, and showed him into the lounge. Jon got up as Nick entered.

'Hello. I'm Jon,' he was unsure whether to offer a handshake and finally decided against it.

'Detective Inspector Nick Price, Cheshire Constabulary. Shall we sit down?'

'Can I offer you a cup of tea?' Chrissy asked, her attitude mellowing somewhat in the light of the sergeant's explanation.

'Not for me, thanks, I've just had lunch. But does

Jon...?'

'No thanks, Mum.'

'Right, I'll let you get on, then,' she said and headed for the garden, where her favourite book waited near the summer house.

'So, how long have you been having driving lessons with Doctor Baker?'

'A few weeks now. And can we call him Gary, everybody did.'

'Was he good?'

'Yes. I thought so. Lots of things to look out for, especially on the country lanes. We did some busy roads as well. We even went to Liverpool through the tunnel.'

'That's a strange thing, to take a learner driver through the tunnel and into the city.'

'He had someone to see and he thought the experience would be good for me.'

'Any idea why he needed to see this other guy?'

'We picked up a suitcase in Liverpool from a guy named Vince.'

'A suitcase? What was in it?'

'I don't know. I never looked inside. But it didn't seem very heavy. After Liverpool we went to Rhyl – Vince gave us the postcode. We met a girl there, I remember her name was Megan, and Gary took the case into the house with her. I stayed in the car. He seemed keen to get away when he came out, just chucked the case in the back and told me to drive.'

'What happened next?'

'I think the case was in the car all weekend because it was still there on the following Tuesday when we went to

Bangor Races to give the case to someone else. Another guy from Liverpool. But he didn't turn up. Two other guys said he'd been delayed and they were to collect the case. Gary didn't like it, but they were in a queue of traffic leaving the racecourse. The cars behind them were blowing their horns and he gave them the case and they left.'

'I bet it was chaotic at the exit. It usually is on race day. All keen to get home or to the pub.' Nick observed.

'Yes, we managed to get out and we had the radio on as we came home and we heard that a body had been found at the racecourse. Gary assumed that the victim was supposed to pick up the case and these other two had killed him. Until then, I didn't know what was in the case, but Gary told me later that there was a lot of money in it and he was worried what Vince would do about it. I think we know, don't we?'

'It looks like it, but we can't go around arresting people on circumstantial evidence. We'll certainly be interviewing Vince about it. Your description ties in with what I knew already. Now are you sure you didn't know about the money until after the races?

'Positive. He said he only took me along as camouflage. How many criminals drive round with L-plates on? Your lot would never suspect a learner. All the drug dealers are in fast cars, aren't they?' Nick grudgingly agreed.

'Did you get a good look at the two who took the case?'

'No. I was sitting in the driver's seat and we were parked next to the lane of traffic leaving the course. Gary had got out of the car so that they would pass us and he could get the case out of the car and into theirs, so he was standing in my way.'

'What about when he went to the back of the car to get the case out?'

'By then, I was looking at the policeman on the road waving the traffic on because they had stopped. Right agitated he was. So I didn't see them at all. Then they shot off in a cloud of dust and Gary got back in the car. All I know was it was a BMW, but most of the cars there were BMW's'

'What colour?'

'Blue, I think.'

'Very popular colour.' Nick had difficulty hiding his disappointment.

Nick felt it was clear that if the contents of the case were worth killing for, then the driver of the BMW wasn't one of Vince's men. But at least he had something to take to Diane Coleman on Merseyside. The post code, which was Vince's address and a blue BMW. It's a start.

'So what are you going to do about driving lessons, now you've lost your private tutor?' he asked, as they waited for the fingerprint officer to arrive.

'I'll have to pay at a proper driving school. It'll be hard to save up, but I've got a part-time job lined up. Starting tonight, in fact.'

'Oh yes. Where at?'

'The Ram's Head Inn. I had a word with Sheryl, Gary's partner and she's short of someone to help out, you know, collect glasses, change barrels, fetching and carrying, that sort of stuff.'

'That'll be interesting. Meeting people, learn the trade, you never know, you could go on and make a real career out of it'

'That's what my Dad says.'

Nick's phone buzzed. After a short conversation he clicked off.

'The fingerprint officer will be a little late. He'll be another half hour, so I'll leave you to wait for him. You won't need me here and I've got other interviews to do. I'll just say goodbye to your Mum. She doesn't seem very happy'

'No, she's been like this for a few days now. It might have been your lot searching the house.'

'In that case I'll definitely have a word to put her mind at rest.' He walked up the garden, appreciating the sunshine.

'Mrs Maitland,' he began, 'I get the feeling that you're upset about something. Was it having your house searched the other day?'

'Well, that didn't help but ...no...it's nothing...I'll be OK'

'It doesn't sound like nothing. Are you sure there isn't something you'd like to tell me? I can be very discreet you know.'

She thought hard. David had said to keep it in the family.

'Oh, I've got to tell somebody. We've had a letter.' The words came out in a rush.

'A letter.'

'Yes. This one.' She took the envelope from between the pages of her book. She had been using it as a book-mark.

'May I read it? Nick asked.

'Please do. We've tried not to touch it. Fingerprints.' She stifled a tear.

Nick opened the envelope and read.

'So who is this directed at? It doesn't say.'

161

'That's the problem. We don't know. It might be me.'

'You? Is there anything you could be blackmailed about?'

She looked towards the house to check Jon's whereabouts

'I've never told anyone this apart from two old school friends. It all goes back to my hen party, eighteen years ago. We were all pretty merry. I'd had a lot to drink and I remember Gary Baker walking with me to the nurses' home. The next thing I remember was waking up next morning in my own bed. Someone had undressed me and put me to bed. Gary was the last person I recall and if he had put me to bed .... I've been so worried that he...he... well, you can guess what I thought. David and I were married that weekend and a few weeks later I found that I was pregnant. For the last eighteen years I have wondered whether Gary could be Jon's father. There was no-one I could ask. When DNA tests became possible, I couldn't ask for one. David would have been immediately suspicious – and angry that I hadn't said anything sooner. Then this arrived. I thought it was from Gary. Short of money again.'

'He'd have to be really short to resort to blackmail to solve his problems, don't you think?'

'People do strange things when they're desperate, don't they?'

'Leave it with me, Mrs Maitland. I'll do what I can to find out. Fingerprints might be our first port of call. And stop worrying. It may just be a prank. Someone playing the fool. I'll be off now. A quick word with Jon on the way.' He placed the letter in an evidence bag and returned to the house to find Jon lying on the settee watching afternoon tv

'A quick word, if I may?'

'Yes.' He muted the tv and turned to Nick.

'Your mum has just told me about the blackmail letter.'

'Dad said not to tell the police. 'Keep it in the family,' he said.'

'It's a bit odd, just addressed to anybody or nobody. Are there any pranks going on at school? Like trolls on the net?'

'Maddy mentioned some fake party invitations on Facebook, but nothing like this.'

'So, what do you make of it?'

'It's strange. When it arrived, we all went quiet, as though it was addressed to each of us.'

'What? You all felt guilty? What did you feel guilty about?'

'Ever since I found out about Gary and the drug money, I thought I was going to be arrested.'

'So, who did you think had sent this letter?'

'Gary, of course. He's the only one who knew the full story. And as Vince wants his money, I thought Gary was desperately trying to get some together, though blackmailing me wouldn't gain him very much.'

'You've explained your involvement in the collecting of the drug money, so stop worrying about being arrested. I'll look into this letter and see what we can do.'

He was thoughtful as he walked to the car. He would need to talk to Doctor Maitland before his wife told him that she had told the police about the letter.

He would go to the hospital after his next interview; it would be interesting to talk to Barry Meadows.

How they knew he was a policeman he never knew.

163

Whether it was an aura that surrounded coppers or whether Copper ID was on the curriculum from primary school upwards, he wasn't sure, but when he walked into the betting shop it was amazing how many punters took a great interest in the posters on the walls or made, face averted, for the seclusion of the toilets. He walked up to Vera's counter, taking out his warrant card .

'I don't know that you need to see this,' he said with a smile, 'judging by the effect I've had.'

'You want Barry?' she asked, not returning his smile.

'Please.'

Before she could turn to the door, Barry emerged and unlocked the door at the side of the counter.

'This way,' he said, 'We can't have you out front. It's bad for business.' and led the way into his office, which still dwelt in the dark and distant past. 'And what can I do for you?' he eased into his chair while Nick was offered a hard wooden chair. Barry didn't encourage visitors to stay long.

Nick wasted no time. 'I'm DI Price of Cheshire Constabulary. What can you tell me about Doctor Gary Baker?'

'How long have you got? The short answer is that he owed me a lot of money and now he doesn't. Well, in this trade, very little is committed to paper. A hand-shake, a man's word is his bond and all that rubbish, it only works when they manage to stay alive and you can threaten them or do a deal which suits both sides. I can't ask Sheryl to pay it. It wasn't her debt. I liked Gary. He usually paid up at the end of the month. He's a doctor, for God's sake. He's earning plenty so I let him run on from time to time. He was generous, when he had money. Call in the Ram's Head when he's there and he's the first to put his hand in his pocket and buy you a drink. But, now and again he has a bad run. He loved to bet but he didn't know when to stop. He thought his next bet would be a winner, and as the debt increased, it had to be a big winner. Foinavon doesn't run every week.'

'Foinavon?'

'Won the Grand National at 100 to 1. 1967. Before your time. So I told him that he owed me a grand and I wanted it paid at the end of the month. Then he tells me he owes somebody in Liverpool ten grand. Ha! You'll have to go to all the nut-houses in Liverpool to find the idiot who'd lend Gary ten grand. Apparently, this guy was getting tough with him, so I was having to take second place in the queue. Me, who's put up with his mad betting for years.'

'So now I have the task of finding out who killed him.' Nick put in.

'Well, it wasn't me. Why would I kill the goose that laid the golden eggs?'

'Except there are no golden eggs, are there? They're all addled.'

'Well, I'd still be a fool to do that. And as I say, I liked the fellow, even if he didn't pay his debts. And he was a damn good doctor, Ask Vera. She says he was marvellous with her lad. No, you can count me out on this one. Now, is there anything else you want to know?'

'No, thanks,' Nick said. 'You've been very helpful.'

He clipped his pen into his notebook and left.

'This is turning into a busy day,' he muttered to himself as he drove round to Aggies. He had rung ahead and checked that Doctor Maitland would be able to see him at short notice. He was in luck.

'What can I do for you this time?' David asked as Nick was shown into his office.

'I saw Jon this afternoon. Thanks for arranging that, by the way. I also noticed that Mrs Maitland was unhappy, strained, almost depressed. Certainly, very quiet. And she told me about the letter.'

'What? I said we should keep it in the family,' David's reaction was immediate.

'There's no need to worry. She was reluctant to tell me about it. I don't think she would have said anything. Put it down to a persuasive policeman. With it being addressed to no-one in particular, she's worrying which of you it is intended for. I'm sure you all are. Don't take this the wrong way, but do you think it might be intended for you?'

David gathered his thoughts. 'Only one thing crossed my mind when it arrived, that Gary had gone one step further than he had before and had resorted to blackmail. Although we had been friends since Medical School, he had always resented my success. He never congratulated me on my promotions or took any interest in the different places I had worked. To be honest, I've often thought that he fancied Chrissy. Something in the way he looked at her. He didn't do anything about it, of course, but I just feel that he was jealous of my success, jealous of my marriage. It came to a head when my father passed away and I was the only one in the room with him. I felt that Gary spotted his chance to incriminate me and the letter was aimed at me. You can imagine my relief when I heard that it was Gary who had stolen the pills. Otherwise it would have looked as though I had stolen them to help my father out of this

166

world. Presumably part of his plan. I'd be glad if you could keep this under your hat for now. I wouldn't want the family to know.'

'I'll do what I can,' Nick said and prepared to leave. It had been a long day. And although he hadn't said as much to them, he now had three more suspects for the hit-and-run. And he hadn't seen Maddy yet, though he thought that she would be the most unlikely suspect.

An evening with Helen would make today perfect. He rang her from the car park. A leisurely stroll along the riverside at Chester would be very relaxing indeed.

TWENTY-EIGHT

'Hi Megan. How's Southport?'

'Fine, thanks, Uncle Mick.'

'Just a quick call. Can you tell me anything else about that contact of Vince's, the one who collected the money?'

'Well, Vince said he was a doctor at the hospital they took him to when he came off his bike. Aggies at Thornhill.'

'Hmm. Middle of Cheshire. Anything else?'

'He had a blue car. He had a learner driving it. He called him Jon; just a lad. Seventeen or eighteen. Didn't seem to know much about what was going on.'

'Probably kept him in the dark. Good policy with kids.'

'That's about all I know, Uncle Mick.'

'OK. Thanks. How's the plastic surgery progressing?

'It'll take a few weeks. First operation is next week. I'll let you know how I get on.'

'Make sure you do. See you soon.'

'Bye.'

Mick Laggan walked out on to the yard. The buildings of his empire stood on three sides of a square, the fourth side being the boundary fence with the huge electric gates that opened on to the road. Visitors arriving through those gates found the offices and reception on their right with the weighbridge beyond. The second side, ahead, was the massive warehouse with room for two lorries to be loaded at the same time from the stacks of pallets which were stored here occasionally. The third side, facing the offices, contained a repair shop, garaging for the company's vans and a washing bay. Mick insisted on each vehicle leaving the yard being in pristine condition. CCTV cameras covered every corner and floodlights overlooked the whole arena – for arena it was. The untutored eye watching the skilful drivers manoeuvring their articulated vehicles would certainly consider it a performance.

As he stood outside the offices, he called across to Eddie and pointed to the warehouse. Eddie nodded and started the engine of a white van which he drove into the warehouse. Mick met him there and closed the double doors behind the van.

Eddie opened the rear doors of his van which was dwarfed by the lorry parked next to it.

'Three for Rod's End Farm,' Mick said. 'You've been there before. It's almost in Shropshire.'

Yeah. I know it. Hour and a half each way. No probs.'

'And Eddie?'

'Yeah?'

'On the way back, call in at Thornhill. Don't be obvious, but pop into the village shop.'

'It won't be open at the time we'll be passing,' Eddie put in.

'OK The pub then. Keep your ears open, see what you can find out about that guy who gave you the money at Bangor. I think he's a doctor. And there's the kid who was driving him. What can you find out about him? But be careful. Keep a tight rein on Robbie. We don't want a repeat of the last time. Remember, you'll be out in the country. People will remember you as strangers, so don't get up to anything.'

'OK Boss.'

Eddie turned to the lorry and opened the rear door.

'Come on. Out.' He beckoned to the occupants, who scrambled out and followed Mick's indications to the back of the white van. Three pairs of wary eyes, fearful of what fate they might be going into. They had travelled across Europe, trusting people all the way. They had paid good money - they knew they were being overcharged, but it was worth it to make it to Britain. They had to trust that they would receive decent treatment when they got here. Every change of transport was a worry. When would the ordeal end? They had been working in the east of England for weeks, now they were moving on.

'Work?' one of them asked Mick as he climbed into the back of the van.

'Yes. Good work.' Mick was reassuring.

Once loaded, doors were closed on the lorry and the van, the warehouse doors opened and Eddie drove the van out, picked up Robbie on the yard and set off. A trip in the country was just what he needed.

He got to Rod's End Farm in reasonable time, delivered the migrant workers, collected Mick's share of the money and made the slight detour to Thornhill on the way back to Liverpool. As they got out of the van in the Ram's Head car park he spoke to Robbie.

'Now remember. Keep your ears open and your mouth shut.'

'But I thought we were having a drink.'

'Don't be funny. Make it a swift half, but leave the talking to me.'

There were about a dozen regulars in at this hour. Conversation buzzed around what they had heard on the 6 o'clock news, latest football results and prospects for the weekend fixtures. In this part of Cheshire there was always a football team you could support, with Liverpool and Manchester within half an hour plus so many lower league teams, vocal rivalry got boisterous at times. In the presence of so many Premiership supporters, Eddie decided to keep his allegiance to Tranmere Rovers under wraps

Sheryl had not returned to work yet so Steve was behind the bar. He was a good stand-in for Sheryl. He gave each customer his full attention while he was serving them, dropping in and out of the general conversation between customers. He spotted Eddie's accent straight away.

'I suppose you'll be a Liverpool supporter, then?' he said, as he passed over the change.

'Nah, Me old dad said never to discuss football, religion or politics, and I think he's right.'

Steve laughed. 'If we banned those, this place would be as quiet as the grave.'

'Aye, I suppose it is quiet out here in the country. Nothing much happens from one day to the next. I'm a townie, myself'. Always something happening in town.'

'We do get a bit of excitement now and again, you know. The other day, we had a hit-and-run. Local chap. Doctor at the hospital. His partner is our manager. Killed outright, he was, on the way home from here. No idea who did it.'

He went to serve another customer and Eddie turned and sat with Robbie at a table facing the bar.

The mention of the hit-and-run changed the subject of the general conversation from football. There was an air of sadness as they had all enjoyed Gary's company in the pub and theories as to who, how and when were put forward

171

and were either squashed or supported.

'Yes, grand chap, Gary.' An old man in the corner passed final judgement. Another spoke to the lad who was busy collecting empty glasses to put them in the washer.

'Wasn't he teaching you to drive, Jon?' he asked.

Jon looked across the room, looking for empty glasses. The newcomers were only half-way through their drinks.

'Yes. He was a very good teacher, too. Even my dad said, and you know how picky he can be. But now he's gone I'm going to have to pay for lessons at a driving school, so Sheryl said I could work here part time.'

Eddie decided it was time to leave, and with a 'Time we were off,' to Steve, they drank up and made for the door.

When they were back in the van, Robbie said 'What's the rush? It was just getting interesting.'

'Too interesting, if you ask me. I think that was the lad who was driving the other car when we went to Bangor... the races... remember? So, I thought if I recognised him, we'd better get out before he recognised us.'

'Perhaps he did but didn't say anything. Or it might dawn on him later on, He wouldn't have seen you as you were driving, but I spoke to the other fellow through the window, he'd have had a good view of me. What we gonna do, Eddie?' There was panic in his voice.

'Calm down, Robbie. He may not have twigged. You're panicking over nothing.'

'It's alright for you. It was me who spiked Terry and we've got away with it so far.'

'Look, we're out of the village now. Let's pull over and think.'

In the next lay-by they parked, switched the lights off

and thought.'

Their thoughts got more and more bizarre, from dropping Jon off the Runcorn Bridge into the river to laying him on the railway line for the next train to silence him for them.

'You're getting too wild, Robbie. Mick said he didn't want a repeat of last time. That means nobody gets killed. He's only a kid. We'll put the frighteners on him. Kidnap him, keep him for a day or so and threaten him a bit with more of the same if he tells the police about us. That should be enough.'

'That's good, Eddie. Wish I'd thought of that.'

They drove quietly back into the village and parked where they could see the door of the Ram's Head and waited. They hadn't come prepared for a kidnapping so they improvised with a scarf of Eddie's which was stuffed behind a seat for a blindfold and a tow rope which Mick insisted all his vehicles carried.

Jon was walking home at the end of his shift, his mind jumping from one subject to another. What a day! Had his fingerprints taken – that was a new experience. Been interviewed by the police. Done his first shift in a pub. His Dad wasn't too keen on that, but agreed that his son needed the money. Jon was so deep in thought that he didn't even notice that he was passing a white van parked in a dark spot where the overhanging trees obscured the street lights. Suddenly, a man appeared from the front of the van, his features indistinguishable in the deep shadows, and held him in a bear hug. From behind, a scarf was wrapped quickly around his face and knotted tightly behind his neck. The bear hug held his arms immobile, then hands behind

173

him pulled his wrists together and a rope was tightened around them. He was lifted off the ground and he heard the doors opening. He was dumped into the back of the van and his feet tied together to stop the wild kicking that was the only resistance he could manage. His attempts to shout an alarm were muffled by the scarf and at that time of night, there was no-one to hear him anyway. Eddie drove quietly out of the sleeping village without drawing attention to the van and returned to Liverpool.

At Mick's yard, he drove into the garage area and parked. The night staff had waved him in and took no further notice of what he was doing.

He switched the van lights off and closed the garage doors. Then with the light from the screen of his mobile phone, he got into the back of the van, lifted the scarf so that Jon could speak and spoke quietly to the boy.

'You're Jon, right?'

'Yes.'

'Do you know why you're here?'

'No. What have I done? What do you want?'

'One question at a time. We're not going to hurt you, yet. Have you been talking to the police?'

'Yes. They took my fingerprints this afternoon because I'd been driving Gary's car and it was used in the hit-and-run. But I didn't do it.' The words came out in a panicky rush.

'Just elimination, then?'

'Yes.'

'Were you driving at Bangor Races the other week?'

'Yes.'

'Well, I want you to forget everything you saw at Bangor

when your friend passed the case over. In fact, it never happened.'

'Why? How are you involved?'

'Let's say, I know the people who took the money in the case and who killed Terry. And they don't want the police to know. So if you don't tell them they won't know. Got it?'

'Yes. But I didn't see anybody.'

'And that's what you tell the police. Now we're going to keep you here for a while to make sure you've got the message. If you make any noise or cause any trouble, we'll change the blindfold for a plastic bag.'

'But I'll suffocate.'

'Exactly. So you know to be nice and quiet.'

Eddie had spoken quietly but the menace in his voice and the threats he made were not lost on his victim. Jon spent an uncomfortable, dreamless night on the floor of the van.

TWENTY NINE

Chief Inspector Tom Cameron met Nick at his office door at 8.30am next morning.

'I don't know what's going on at Thornhill but you seem to have a crime wave starting up there. You'll have to keep on top of it.'

'I thought we were making progress, sir,' Nick replied. 'The missing pills case has been closed, I have three more suspects for the hit-and-run....'

'And you've now got a missing person. Doctor Maitland has been on this morning to say his son hasn't been home all night. You'd better get over there and see what it's all about.'

He left his boss's office and thoughts ran through his mind as he walked to the car park. It was no good trying to explain that teenage boys were a law unto themselves. Perhaps he'd got a girl-friend. Perhaps he'd gone home with a mate and had an impromptu sleep-over because it got too late to go home - all sorts of reasons. You would have thought that the Maitlands were more level-headed than to get in a panic when a big lad like Jon stayed out all night. However, the boss had spoken. He got into his car and drove to Thornhill.

'Ah, you're here at last.' David Maitland was hardly welcoming as he walked down the drive to meet Nick, who had just arrived.

'Good morning,' Nick glossed over the veiled criticism in the doctor's welcome. 'My Chief Inspector tells me that Jon failed to come home last night. Shall we discuss it in the house? I'm sure Mrs Maitland would like to know what's

176

going on as well. And is Maddy about? She may know something.'

'They are both indoors. We'll join them in the lounge.'

Nick found himself sitting on the settee where he had last seen Jon, watching afternoon tv. Mrs Maitland sat in the armchair, twisting a tear-soaked handkerchief in her lap. On the arm of the armchair sat a pale, worried Maddy, to be close to her mother. David Maitland, looking impatient at having to sit still instead of physically looking for his son, occupied the armchair on the other side of the fireplace.

'Perhaps I ought to say, first of all, that this is early to start a missing person enquiry, in that most missing persons turn up within twenty-four hours, having gone missing for quite innocent reasons, just thoughtlessness about letting the family know their plans. So, please don't think that we are treating this lightly if you feel there's a lack of urgency in our approach to the problem. So, is Jon likely to have stayed with a friend last night?'

'No, he would have rung to let us know.' Chrissy sprang to the defence of her son.

Nick pressed on, 'Maddy, could you give me the names of some of his mates, so I can check?'

'Duncan Baker was the only one he might have gone to.'

'Doctor Baker's son?'

'Yes.'

'Good. I have his address.'

'We've already rung Sheryl, but we had to leave a message on the answer-phone.' Chrissy put in

'He told me yesterday that he was starting a job at the Ram's Head last night. Did he go?

'Yes. He left here about five thirty and was due to finish

work at ten.' Chrissy said. 'It's so unlike him. He's always been considerate and let us know if he's going to be late.'

'I'll go round there; my first port of call. The bar staff won't be in till later. I doubt if the cleaners will know anything that happened last night, so it's no good ringing now. It might seem a silly question, but are you sure his bed hasn't been slept in?'

'Yes, we've checked.' David was short and definite with his answer, obviously impatient for the detective to get on with searching for his son.

'All his clothes are still here? What about money. Is he likely to have much on him?'

'Yes to the clothes and no to the money. Why would that be important?'

'If he was planning to go away somewhere there could be taxi fares, rail fares, food. It's as well for me to establish a picture now rather than keep running back at each new development. He seemed keen on this job when I spoke to him yesterday; he didn't have any disagreements with any of you after I left?

Chrissy replied 'No, he was, as you say, looking forward to the job when he left. I'm so worried. What with Gary getting killed...I can't help thinking it's connected.'

Maddy slipped off the arm of her mother's chair and went into the kitchen. Nick heard her moving one or two items on the shelves before she returned.

'What was that all about?' her father asked.

'I had a thought,' she replied. 'The key to Gary's car, the one Jon used, isn't where he kept it. Could he have taken the car?'

'It's not possible,' Nick said. 'The car is in our

workshops with the key still in it. Thanks for thinking about it.' He smiled his appreciation. At least Maddy was being constructive even if her father wasn't. 'By the way, Maddy, if you think of any other friends he might have gone to, you can text me the details and I'll go to see them.' He gave her his card and turned to Chrissy.

'I'm going now. You're not to start worrying, Mrs Maitland. It's early days. I'm sure you'll let me know if he turns up in the meantime.' He gave her his card and left, with an assurance to David that he would keep them informed at every step of the way.

At the same time as the Chief Inspector was meeting Nick on his arrival at work, Mick Laggan was calling his henchman into his office.

'Right, Eddie. You've got my money from Rod's End, I take it?

'Yes, here you are, Mick,' as he handed over a thick envelope, 'It's all there.'

'Thanks, Eddie. A bit more for the pension fund. How did you get on at Thornhill last night?'

'OK, really.'

'The reason I ask, your tracker showed some funny patterns on the map. You were leaving Thornhill, then you went back in, then you turned around and parked up on the residential part on the road out again and then you returned back here, very late. You must have put the key to the garage in your pocket because I can't get in there this morning. So what's going on?'

'We went to the pub, as you suggested, just a swift half and guess what?'

'No. You tell me.'

'There was a kid collecting glasses in there and he was the same one who was driving the other car at Bangor races. You said it was a small world. Well, I thought, if I recognise him, he might recognise me or Robbie, so we drank up and left, and the more we thought about it, it seemed obvious that we ought to make sure he didn't tell anyone about us, so we've got him tied up in the back of the van. I kept the garage key to make sure none of the mechanics went in there before I got here this morning.'

'Bloody hell! What did you intend to do with him? That's kidnapping. You can go down for that. And now you've involved me. You haven't thought this out, have you?'

'He's only a kid, so a couple of nights in the van might convince him that we're serious, and I'll take him back and let him go tomorrow night. A dose of the frighteners will do him good. He doesn't know who we are and I made sure Robbie' didn't give us away.'

'Sounds barmy to me, but it may work. But take him back tonight, we don't want to keep him too long. And we don't want any of the mechanics going in there and finding him. Take the van round to my lock up on Nesbit Street, out of harm's way. '

'Right, Mick. I'll take him back to Thornhill after dark, in case you feel like tracking me again.'

'No need to get sarcastic. It's for your own good.'

Jon had spent an uncomfortable night on the floor of the van. Trussed as he was in an awkward position, he was unable to stretch or flex. Still blindfolded, he had no idea of night or morning. His only guide to time was when he heard voices echoing from another building, voices which he assumed were people starting a day's work. Car engines as workers arrived; lorry engines as the work commenced; all the noises of a busy yard. He heard doors being unlocked, footsteps going to the front of the van, then the engine fired up and he felt the motion of the van moving slowly backwards, then accelerating forwards then turning sharply, causing Jon to roll, then roll back to his original position as the van straightened up and joined what Jon assumed was heavy traffic, from the sounds he could hear. The van stopped. There were footsteps receding. Footsteps returning. The journey was resumed, A sudden right-angled turn threw Jon over again, followed by a sudden stop. He heard the sound of an up-and-over door being lifted and the van drove into what he assumed was a garage. The garage door was closed and the back door of the van was opened.

'Just checking you're alright,' Eddie said, without checking anything more than that Jon was still alive.

'I'm cold, stiff and hungry.' Jon's voice was muffled by the scarf around his face.

'You'll be OK till later,' Eddie said, impervious to Jon's condition, then closed the van door and failed to hear a pained 'And thirsty!' from Jon. He closed the garage door. His receding footsteps were followed by silence.

Jon twisted again for what seemed, to him, like the millionth time, to release the knots which held the ropes tight to his bleeding wrists. He had no feeling in his feet, he was suffering in so many ways in addition to cold, stiff, hungry and thirsty. But why? Something to do with Gary and the suitcase at Bangor, but what? It was so unfair. All he had done was drive. He knew nothing of the purpose of their errand. Was Gary's hit-and-run really an accident? If these men had killed Gary, what had they got planned for him? They had killed Terry, the intended contact at Bangor. No wonder they didn't care about his welfare. 'OK till later' the man had said. What happens later? The threat of a plastic bag loomed large in his mind. It was a long wait to find out.

THIRTY

During the morning, Nick had contacted both Sheryl and Steve, her barman, but neither could provide any help or guidance as to Jon's whereabouts or his plans the night before. Steve reported that the only customers who were not regulars were two Liverpool lads who came in for a swift half and left – in rather a hurry, he thought – but they didn't seem to take any special interest in Jon while they were in the pub. The Liverpool connection wasn't lost on Nick and he wanted to know more about their visit. Steve could only remember a few details.

'They were in for about ten minutes. They came in... just a minute.' he searched his memory. '.it would have been just before eight o'clock, because they passed Laurie Preston in the doorway on their way out. and he always arrives at five past eight. You can set your clock by him.'

'Why five past eight? Sounds odd.' Nick was interested.

'He can't miss Coronation Street and that finishes at eight. He lives round the corner.'

'Makes sense, I suppose.' Nick said, then asked 'Do you have CCTV in here?'

'Yes. You have to, these days. You never know when you are going to get sued, so you have to cover yourself.

'I'd like to see last night's footage, if you don't mind.'

'Not at all.' Steve was keen to help and led the way into the cubby-hole under the stairs which served as the office. He pointed out the split screen showing six cameras.

'There you are, help yourself,' he said, and left Nick to watch the previous night's proceedings.

It was interesting. Nick watched the interaction between

the regulars as the evening progressed. How people by-passed one chair to sit on another, for the by-passed chair to be filled by its regular occupant later on. Everyone had their favourite seat. Just before ten to eight on the counter, two strangers came in. Obviously strangers, by the way they looked around, got their bearings and selected their seats. Two half-pints were served with some banter with the barman. Nick then recognised Jon going round to collect glasses and wipe tables. The two strangers got up and seemed to be hurrying to leave. True to form, Laurie Preston met them in the doorway as they made their exit. It was five past eight. Switching to the outside camera, Nick saw them getting into a white van, but, to his great disappointment, the camera did not pick up the number plate as it left the car park; it was obscured by a low wall. Nick thought to check what time Jon had left the pub. Hadn't Steve said that Jon was on till ten? He was back on the split screen with a view of all six cameras and scrolled on to nine forty five. He could see Jon rushing round, clearing tables. There would be much more clearing up to do by twelve o'clock when the pub closed, but that was Steve's problem. Jon's shift finished at ten. Nick's eye was caught by a movement on the outside camera. A white van, which entered the car park, turned around and left the way it had come. Again, there was no decent view of the number plate. Nick re-ran this section, but gained nothing by which he could identify this van from the million-and-one other white vans on the roads; no names, no rust patches, no broken handles. Flicking back and forth between five past eight and nine forty five he compared the views of the white van. As far as he could tell, it was the

184

same van.

The white van's arrival and departure was corroborated by the cameras at the Cumberland Arms, which Nick visited next, and though their cameras were sited further from the road, a white van passing at times just before and just after its visits to the Ram's Head was clearly in view. Unfortunately, there were no other businesses along that stretch of road and householders who had installed CCTV only covered the area immediately surrounding their home, with no view of the road, thanks to the generous expanse of front garden with mature trees and high hedges outside each house.

Convinced now that the white van was involved in Jon's disappearance and that the Liverpool connection was a valid source of enquiry, he checked the possible routes which the van would have taken if, indeed, it had returned to Liverpool. They could have followed the M53 up the Wirral to the Kingsway Tunnel, the A41 to Birkenhead and the Queensway Tunnel or the M56, turning at Junction 12 for Runcorn and then Speke.

He explained all this to DI Diane Coleman at Merseyside HQ during his next call and wondered if Diane could use her influence to get the tunnel police to trawl through their CCTV at appropriate times; ANPR would be a big help. At least they had approximate times to make the job easier.

'I can try,' said Diane, 'though what influence you think I might have with the tunnel police might not be enough. It would help if we knew which part of Liverpool was their intended destination.'

'That we don't know, unfortunately. It seems that this

case is getting more complicated by the minute and there is more Liverpool involvement than we thought. It might be useful to pool our information or two of us might end up chasing the same people. The murder at Bangor Racecourse also had a Liverpool element and DI Dave Tudor in North Wales is working on that. What would you say to the three of us meeting up at, say, Chester to see what we can do to clear the log jam?'

'OK by me, Nick. Set it up with Dave and ring me with possible dates. The sooner the better.'

Nick repeated this conversation with DI Dave Tudor, who also agreed that an early meeting would be useful.

'What about 4 o'clock this afternoon? I'm less than half an hour away.'

'OK by me, I'll ring Diane and see if she's free.'

His call to Diane Coleman got the confirmation he wanted. All three were to meet at Chester Police HQ, Nick having got the approval of Chief Inspector Tom Cameron for the use of an interview room.

THIRTY ONE

After lunch, Chrissy made her way to her mother's bungalow, having left Maddy at home with strict instructions to ring immediately in case of any developments. It had been a few days since she had seen Alex and had been concerned at the deterioration in her mother's health. She had lost weight, which Alex had explained away by golf and dieting – to make sure she got into a new dress for the golf club Summer Ball, she said. She was not as lively as she had been, but Alex put it down to age. 'I'm still very active, but Anno Domini takes its toll, you know' she said. None of this fooled Chrissy, and she now had another reason to make a visit – other than checking on Alex's health. For her part, Alex knew that the time was coming ever closer that she would have to desist from such flimsy excuses and tell the family of her terminal cancer. It had been quite a few weeks since Jim Parton had said 'weeks rather than months.'

Alex met Chrissy at the door. 'Shall we sit in the garden? It's such a lovely day. I've made some fresh orange juice. Would you like a glass? I'll get some from the kitchen.' and turned into the bungalow without waiting for a reply. Chrissy noticed the almost nervous machine gun rattle of the questions, as though Alex was reluctant to leave a gap for her daughter to ask a question. She took a seat on the patio and Alex returned with two glasses, ice cubes clinking on the sides. Chrissy sipped her drink and approved. 'Lovely!' she said.

'Have you heard anything from Jon yet? When you phoned me this morning you didn't give me any details.

What's happened?'

'Well, mother. Jon didn't come home last night and nobody knows where he is.' The end of the sentence was dissolved in tears. She was finding it difficult to imagine anything other than the worst. She went on, 'I couldn't explain on the phone. I just needed to check whether he was here. He started a new job at the Ram's Head last night. He finished work at ten and Steve the barman said he was OK when he left. But he didn't get home and...' More tears left a gap – but Alex could fill in the end of the sentence herself.

'It's a worry, I know. But you must be optimistic, dear. There's probably a straightforward explanation, you know what boys are.'

'But he's always let me know if he's going to be late. There's no reply from his phone. The police are looking for him, though they're not too worried yet. They think he'll turn up just like that, all innocent. I was hoping he had spent the night here, with you, though I would have expected a phone call from one of you if that had happened.'

'Well, of course I would have rung if he had turned up here, but he didn't. Strange things are happening. It all started when he got involved with Gary Baker. He was enjoying his driving lessons, too. Did he tell you I was giving him my car?'

'Yes, Mum. He said something about you getting a lift to the course with your golf partner.'

'I need a rest from driving. I know I've always said that I'll keep on driving till the end, but I find it tiring and Sally is just down the road, she will take me to golf – and anywhere else I want to go, so it seemed logical to let Jon have the car. He may as well get as much enjoyment out of it as he can. I'm sure he'll look after it.'

'Rest assured, David will make sure he does that. But I must get back home in case the police ring with news. I'm so worried. It can't be thoughtlessness that he hasn't rung to let me know what's happening. Something horrible, I'm sure. So - I can't stop. Must be off.'

She finished her drink, gathered her handbag, which she slung over her shoulder, and made for the door.

Her mother decided not to bring up the subject of her failing health at the moment. The fact that Chrissy had not even enquired after her mother's health showed that she had enough on her plate with Jon's disappearance. Her health could wait, but not for long. She stood on the doorstep as Chrissy left.

'Bye, darling. Give me a ring as soon as you have news.'

'I will, Mum. Bye for now.'

And she was gone.

THIRTY TWO

The three Detective Inspectors sat around a polished table. As Nick had called the meeting, he assumed Chairmanship and thanked the other two for coming at such short notice.

'We all have cases on the go which seem to have things in common, so I suggest each of us describes their current progress and perhaps we can make some useful connections. Agreed?'

The others nodded.

'Shall I go first?' he asked and again had their approval.

'My case is a hit-and-run. A local doctor, Gary Baker, was killed, we think deliberately, Oddly, it was his own car, which we found in the car park of Green Shoots Garden Centre. Unfortunately, in their efforts to add to the character of the car park, the management installed low hedges and decorative raised flower beds all over the place, which obscured number plates. The driver used this to his advantage so we have no clue as to the identity of the perpetrator's car, to which he transferred after leaving Doctor Baker's car. Doctor Baker was walking home from the Ram's Head Inn with his partner, Sheryl Manton and he was struck between the Ram's Head and the Cumberland Arms. Sheryl also fell in the melée and only had a glimpse of the driver. She said he had white hair. So who would want Doctor Baker dead?'

'We know Doctor Baker had money troubles. He owed the local bookmaker, Barry Meadows, a thousand pounds. He was the kind of gambler whose next bet was going to be the big win which would change his life. This never, if ever, happens, as we know. He had also told Meadows that he owed ten grand to someone in Liverpool, someone who was likely to get rough if he didn't get his money. We now know his name is Vince Spivey.'

'If I can now jump back in time, to a couple of months ago. He had agreed to give driving lessons to the son of a colleague, Doctor David Maitland. They both worked at Thornhill Hospital, and Doctor Baker was being blackmailed by Spivey, who had been a patient at the hospital, into stealing some morphine, which he did. This laid him open to being coerced into driving to Rhyl to collect drug takings on Spivey's behalf. He therefore used his driving lessons to hide the purpose of his journey. The Maitland boy, Jon, by the way, was entirely unaware of what they were doing. So Baker collected the takings, ten grand, and was to hand it to a colleague of Spivey's at Bangor Racecourse. We have all heard of the murder at Bangor. The victim was Baker's contact, but two other men collected the money – they said it was for Spivey but they worked for someone else, unknown at the moment. Presumably, they killed Spivey's courier to achieve the robbery. Young Jon Maitland said one of them spoke with a Liverpool accent. They drove off in a blue BMW. He didn't get the number, and looking for a blue BMW is like looking for a man in a red shirt at Anfield on a Saturday afternoon. Anything you can add here, Dave?'

Dave Tudor was in his late forties, his youthful blond hair slowly turning to grey, but there was still plenty of it. He brushed it back as he opened his file. 'Nick's description of the goings-on at Bangor is spot on, and we have failed to find anyone who fits the bill. There were rear views of

191

presumably the killers on the CCTV but nothing conclusive – until I re-read a report on his afternoon's duty from a constable who was on traffic duty that day. He was on the gate directing traffic as it left at the end of racing. He noted a hold-up at one point and waved them on to keep the stream moving. Someone was passing a suitcase from a parked car next to the ropes to a blue BMW, which then left at speed. The driver even waved a 'thank you' to him as they passed him. He had no chance of taking a number, but he did notice a skull and cross bones sticker in the back window. I'm hoping that will enable us to identify the car and its occupants. All we know at this stage is that one of them had a Liverpool accent.'

Diane Coleman was writing as he spoke. 'I'll get Traffic on to it as soon as I get back.' she said, and went on. 'If I can add to Dave's case, on the evening of Bangor races, a car was left in the car park. It had been driven by the murder victim and obviously was the last car in the car park. It was traced to a Vince Spivey and he was visited by a couple of our PC's that evening to report that it had been found. His story was that he had lent it to a mate. Sounds plausible, but he's hardly going to mention collecting ten grands-worth of drug money to us, is he? We've asked him if he had any idea who might have killed his mate but he said 'No, he's probably got into a fight and it's all gone wrong for him.' Again, we don't believe him, but if it's a rival gang he'll be wanting to settle the score himself. Now we know about the drug money, we're keeping a closer watch on Mr Spivey.'

'Thanks for that, Diane,' Dave Tudor said. 'If anything comes up about the Rhyl connection, we'll be glad to check it out for you.'

'Thank you, both. It's great to see co-operation actually working. Now, there's more to say on my case,' Nick said.

'Just before Gary Baker was killed, The Maitland family received a blackmail letter, anonymous, of course, with a hint that a request for money could be following. All four thought it was aimed at them personally for things that the rest of this respectable family didn't know about. I've spoken to all of them and they each suspect that Gary Baker was the author, trying to get money to pay off his debts. So that gives me four suspects for the hit-and-run. Then there's Barry Meadows, the bookmaker, Vince Spivey and the boys in the BMW.'

'Why them?' Diane asked.

'They could be worried that he could identify them for the murder of Spivey's mate.

'Of course, good point. A strong motive. So how many does that make?'

'Eight. I've tried scoring them on their likelihood of being the guilty party.'

'How does that go?' Dave wanted to know.

'To start with the family, they all had access to the ignition key of the car. Jon usually kept it on a shelf in the kitchen. Now, David Maitland, the father, had a row with Gary, who suggested that David had administered drugs to his dying father. His position at the hospital would be untenable if that came out, whether it's true or not. I'd score him six or seven. Chrissy Maitland, mother, is worried that Gary may turn out to be Jon's father, a secret she has lived with for eighteen years since getting drunk at her hen party. I don't see her as a murderer, so she scores four or even less, but she could have hired someone to do it. Jon Maitland, seventeen, is afraid he'll be charged with drug offences after his driving with Gary. He is, at present, nowhere to be found. Just vanished off the scene, which makes me highly suspicious. Perhaps he's done a runner. I score him nine. Maddy, sixteen, was filmed dancing in her underwear. She thinks her father would be outraged if it went on social media. Gary knew about it. However, she was the one who pointed out that the key was kept in the kitchen and went to look for it when I was there. Either she's a brilliant actress and is worthy of a high score or she was innocently honest. I think the latter. Score one. Barry Meadows, bookmaker, owed a thousand pounds, score two. He wouldn't kill for that amount. Spivey, ten grand down, must be spitting feathers. His taxi business is not big enough to maintain his lifestyle. He has a Goldwing and now we know that he was into drugs. If that ten grand was a week's takings, he's into it big time. I'd describe him as ruthless. Score eight, possibly nine. BMW boys. Killed already. Must be worried that Gary could identify them. Ten.'

'That's a fair assessment,' was Diane's comment. 'We'll give you what help we can, looking for the BMW etcetera'.

.'That would be very useful,' Dave Tudor said, 'I think there's some hope of success now we have an idea of the suspects. With this in mind, I'd like to interview Spivey myself – no disrespect to your boys, Diane ' (a dismissive wave from Diane) 'but I'll restrict myself to my murder case. If I hear anything which points to his drug sales, I'll pass it on. Mr Spivey won't know what's hit him, two police forces on his tail. He'll be so dizzy he'll probably let something slip.'

'Let's hope so,' Nick said. 'Now this is all happening on Diane's patch, so I propose that she will be our information centre. Everything Dave and I do and hear will be reported to Diane and she will keep us informed of anything she thinks will help us along the way. There may be things that Dave and I would miss but Diane's local knowledge would spot straight away. My first job will be to look for the boys in the BMW. I scored them a ten, so they're high on my list. Spivey may give us a lead, if it was a rival gang; if he does, Dave, let Diane know right away so I can follow it up.' (A confirmatory nod from Dave.) 'On the other hand, Diane, your Traffic team may come up with an ID on the skull and cross bones, in which case I'd like to know. I think you've got the picture. And in the meantime, I can continue investigations in Cheshire and clear some of the names off my list.'

The meeting closed with general agreement on the plan which would enable them to clear up the jigsaw puzzle of crimes.

THIRTY THREE

The van was on the move again and Jon was rolled about as it was driven erratically through what seemed to its reluctant passenger like a maze of T-junctions. At each one, the driver slowed for sufficient time to assess the oncoming traffic, then took a violent turn to left or right, which flung the boy in a different direction. Jon had spent the whole day cooped up, trussed up. not knowing the time, not seeing the daylight, not hearing a human voice. Now he feared the worst. There had been no thought for his welfare during his ordeal. They had already killed Terry. Perhaps they had killed Gary. What fate did they have in store for him?

Then, due to the lack of violent turns, he guessed that they were out of the city environment, and sensed that they were on a straight road, probably a motorway, and were travelling at speed. At least he wasn't being bumped about, a painful process when he was unable to take evasive action to avoid knees, elbows or head coming into serious contact with the floor or walls of his prison. The smooth ride could almost be described as pleasant. Almost.

A couple of roundabouts in quick succession brought him down to earth, as once more he was rolled right and left across the van floor. More pain. A warm, moist feeling told him that his head had been cut. One more full circle in which the centrifugal force pinned him against the wall – had they turned back? A fleeting snatch of music above the engine noise, then back to high revs and high speed.

The sudden stop propelled Jon the full length of the van to fetch up, painfully, against the bulkhead. The back door was opened and rough hands took hold and dragged him to the rear. He felt fresh air on his face at last but there was no time to enjoy it as he was dumped at the side of the road.

At last, a voice. The same voice that had spoken to him before. 'Remember. You know nothing. Unless you'd like to do this again. Only next time, we won't bring you back. Alive, that is.'

Doors slammed. The engine revved up and was gone.

Miss Doris Bellingham was a stalwart of the village. A spinster of three score years and ten plus a few, she was born in Tudor Cottage and lived there still, with a cat and her dog Patch, who was white with the customary patch over one eye. She had served nearly every village duty in her long life. Postmistress, Girl Guide Commisioner, Parish Councillor - a committee wasn't a committee unless Doris was a member of it. But she was not a busy-body. She knew most of her fellow villagers by name and was always available to help, whether it was making hot lunches for the Age Concern group or polishing the brass at the church.

It was no surprise, therefore, when taking Patch for his nightly exercise, that she came across what she thought was a bundle of rags on the pavement. Patch investigated, growled and barked briefly at the bundle, which seemed to growl in return. Doris switched on her torch and made her own investigation and removed the scarf which covered the face of the man who was lying there, trussed and blindfolded. She recognised Jon immediately, took out her mobile phone and dialled 999, ignoring Jon's efforts to say 'No police'.

'I'll ring your father as well,' she said, 'What's his

197

number?'

Jon told her and she dialled it, and it was only a matter of minutes before David and Chrissy arrived from one direction and a police car with blue lights flashing arrived from the other. By now, Jon had been released from his bonds, with the help of Miss Bellingham and was trying to restore the circulation in his limbs which had borne the brunt of his restrictions.

Paramedics arrived and David stood back to allow them to make their assessment. 'I think he'll need to go to hospital, don't you?' was his gentle hint to which they readily agreed, having recognised him from the hospital. Chrissy was concerned to know what had happened and where he'd been and who was responsible, a million-and-one questions which she tried to ask all at once.

David had a word with the policeman, explaining that DI Nick Price would be interested in this and it might be advisable to get him in at this stage. 'Tell him we'll meet him at the hospital,' he said.

When Nick walked into the side room of Ward 10, Jon was already sitting up, surrounded by his family. David had arranged for a bowl of soup to be brought in from the restaurant and Jon was doing it justice.

'Take your time, it's hot,' Chrissy had advised, but Jon reminded her that he hadn't eaten for twenty-four hours and continued to drink ravenously.

'I'll slow down for the second bowl,' he grinned, obviously feeling better already. The resilience of youth. He offered up his empty bowl to one of the many volunteers who make it possible for hospitals to run smoothly, who took it and rushed off to obtain a refill.

A relieved Chrissy had brought down a clean set of clothes for her son; his soiled ones had been put into a black bag for burning. Another job for the volunteer who was secretly enjoying the excitement of Jon's safe return, one of the top doctors here as a parent, police on the ward, a party atmosphere, she would have such stories to tell when she got home.

Nick, on the other hand, had a job to do and, as diplomatically as he could, he cleared the room so that he could interview Jon without interruption and before the story became embellished with things that only happened in Jon's mind.

'So, Jon. Tell me, in your own words, what has happened to you since finishing work at the Ram's Head. Take your time.'

'Not much to tell, really. I was walking along the road and at the spot where I was found, there was a white van, parked, no lights. As I passed it, a man stepped out in front of me and held me in a bear hug. Someone else came up behind me and tied my hands together. They wrapped something, a scarf, I think, around my face and lifted me into the van and drove off. They left me in the van overnight and all next day, no food, not even a drink, then they brought me back and left me where they picked me up. Miss Bellingham took the scarf off and rang my dad and the police and here I am.'

Nick could see that this was the bare bones of a much fuller story which Jon was reluctant to divulge. He would have to probe carefully so as not to put Jon on edge. Keep him relaxed. He pointed to the dressing on Jon's head.

'I bet that was painful. How did it happen?'

'Must have bumped it in the van. I was rolling about a bit and with my hands tied I couldn't protect myself.'

'Rolling about?'

'Yes. Every turn, junctions, roundabouts, I was just flung about.'

'And they left you in the van all day?'

'Yes. Complete darkness. I was blindfolded. Nobody came near me; it was completely silent after they moved me.'

'Moved you?'

'The first journey, from here, was a long one, probably an hour, I guess. I think part of it was on a motorway because it was smooth and I didn't get thrown about. Then we got to wherever it was and they left me, I'd guess it was overnight. I must have been in a garage because I heard people trying the door and then going away without opening it. I tried shouting, but there was too much noise outside from engines starting up. Nobody heard me. Then the van was moved to somewhere else where it was quiet. Not a sound from outside. Then I was brought back home.'

'And what was that journey like?'

'Rough at first. Lots of stops and turns, left and right, then it was smooth for a long time, open road again, I suppose. That was about an hour, but I was losing track of the time. Just before they dropped me off there was one three-sixty degree turn. That hurt. I heard some music for a moment, then it was all over.'

'An hour's journey from here would take you to Liverpool, Manchester and a hundred places in between. Needles and haystacks come to mind.'

Jon wanted to deflect attention from his experiences.

'Well, I'm back safe now. What does it matter where I've been?'

'We take kidnapping very seriously in this country, Jon. It seems you were lucky to be relatively unharmed, but we can't allow people to go round snatching other people in the middle of the night, can we? What would you be saying to me if it was Maddy who had been snatched?'

This put a different complexion on things. Perhaps he had better be more co-operative.

'Hmm. I suppose…'

'What do you suppose?'

'I think it might have been Liverpool. A few weeks ago, Gary took me to Liverpool and we went through the tunnel. It sounds different in there and I heard the same sound on this journey, so it must have been Liverpool.'

'Thanks. That's a positive start. What else do you remember?'

He was wary, not wishing to give too much information. If his captors could pick him up that easily first time, they could do it again. He hadn't forgotten the warning.

'Nothing, really. Just darkness, silence and pain.'

'Didn't anyone speak to you? I'm surprised they didn't tell you why they'd kidnapped you.'

Jon tensed a little and passed a hand across his face. Getting to the hard questions. He thought he'd done well so far, but Eddie's threat was still ringing in his ears.

'No. They didn't speak to me. I could hear voices when we were travelling but they were muffled by the engine noise. I couldn't tell what they were saying. When someone was rattling the door, I assume next morning, one voice said 'Eddie must have the key' before they walked off. Does

201

that help?'

'It will do, if only for confirmation, if we ever find out which of the thousands of Eddies in Liverpool drives a van. Sorry, I'm not being flippant. Of course it will help. Little things often become the most important. So, well done on the recall. Anything else you can think of?'

'There's the scarf that Miss Bellingham took off my face. Mum put it in the bag with my clothes. Dad gave it to the volunteer to take to the incinerator.'

Nick leapt to his feet. 'I'll be back!' he said, and rushed from the room to the nurses' station at the end of the ward.

'Where's the bag?' he asked the nurse.

'Bag? What bag?' She was naturally puzzled.

'The black bag with Jon's clothes. Doctor Maitland gave it to the volunteer to take to the incinerator.'

'It's gone. She took it straight down there.'

'We need to stop her. How do I find her?'

'Halfway down the corridor. Door twelve on your left. I'll ring ahead.'

Nick hardly heard the last words as he went into the corridor and ran at top speed to find Door Twelve. Two more doors were negotiated, creating a lock to isolate the heat and noise of the boilers from the hygiene of the hospital. He burst into the boiler room and a tall man in yellow overalls approached him, hands out in front, saying 'Stop! You're not allowed….' Nick interrupted him, waving his warrant card,

'The black bag. The one the volunteer brought in just now. Where is it?'

'Who's asking?' He was still unsure of Nick's status.

'Police. Inspector Price. We need that bag for evidence,'

'Well why didn't you say? They rang from the ward to tell us to keep it here. They didn't say why, but here it is, safe and sound. Another five minutes and it would have been in the incinerator.'

Nick marvelled at the change in the man's attitude. It's not every day he was called upon to help the police. Evidence, eh? Wonder what the crime was? A bag of clothes. Bloodstains, perhaps. Must be important for an Inspector to run down the corridor. He'd have a story for the lads in the pub tomorrow. He held the door open for Nick to depart.

There you are, sir.' he said.

Nick glanced at his identity badge.

'Thank you, Eric. You did well to save it for me.'

'My pleasure, Inspector Price.' And this time he saluted as the door swung shut behind Nick.

Back in Jon's room, Nick rummaged in the bag, the strong smell of ammonia making his eyes water, and pulled out a blue-and-white scarf. He unrolled it to reveal the words.

'Tranmere Rovers.' he read. 'That's a blessing.'

'Why's that?' Jon asked.

'Think how many suspects we would have had if it had been a Liverpool scarf. This will help us later on, I'm sure.'

Nick felt that the ordeal plus the excitement of his release had taken it out of Jon and he said that he would pop in tomorrow to see if the boy had remembered anything else, and left for the patient to spend a comfortable night.

THIRTY FOUR

Dave Tudor of North Wales Police knocked on the door of a terraced house in Liverpool. As he waited for a response, he studied the outside of the row of identical houses Most were well-kept, with white window frames on their bay windows and doors painted in a kaleidoscope of colours. Even the front walls of these homes were painted from the same imaginative palette. Surprisingly, not many were in the red or blue of the local teams, perhaps to avoid reprisals when emotions were running deep after a derby match had finished with a contentious result. He looked over his shoulder to the grandstand of Goodison Park towering over the surrounding buildings, dwarfing the houses, even a church as they stood in its shadow.

The door opened and Vince Spivey was immediately suspicious to see a stranger standing there. His attention was fixed on the warrant card which was held before his face.

'Good afternoon, Mr Spivey. I'm Detective Inspector Tudor from North Wales police. I'd like a chat, if I may.'

'What have I got to do with North Wales? Are you allowed to come out of your parish?'

'Crime is crime these days, Mr Spivey and we can follow up our cases anywhere. And your car was left at Bangor Racecourse. I'd just like to tie up some loose ends with you.'

'You'd better come in, then.'

Dave followed Vince into the front room of the house. It was tidy and well furnished with the inevitable huge TV screen in the corner. A cocktail bar in the other corner displayed a collection of bottles which included a Metaxa

Brandy, Schnapps, Raki, Sake, Calvados and Ouzo, as well as the standard gin, whisky and vodka. Mr Spivey was obviously a well-travelled man. You didn't need his passport to see that.

'Impressive display' Dave said, nodding towards the bar.

'Just a few things I picked up on holiday,' Vince replied and indicated with a sweep of the hand that they should sit.

Dave Tudor opened the conversation.

'Did you get your car back safely from Bangor, Mr Spivey?'

'Yes, thanks'

'It was very sad about your friend. Were you close?'

'Closer than brothers. My mum took him in when his mother died, so we grew up together.'

'So, very sad indeed. How come you didn't go to the races with him?'

'I wasn't struck on the horses, never have been, and I had a broken leg, so it wouldn't have been much fun.'

'True, but he had another errand, too, didn't he, picking up something else for you?'

'Oh, yes. A suitcase of clothes. From my ex-girl friend. We had parted company and I couldn't collect the clothes I had left with her, so I had them collected for me.'

'That was by Doctor Baker, wasn't it? Surely a strange thing for a doctor to do.'

'Yes, I suppose so.'

'How did you get him to do it?'

"After my crash I was in his hospital. We got talking, as you do and he told me he was teaching a young lad to drive. He was getting fed up with doing the same old lanes out in the country and I joked with him that he ought to try city driving. Well, one suggestion brought another and I asked if he could collect my suitcase for me. He jumped at the chance and it all went well until Bangor Races. Gary, that's Doctor Baker, liked a bet, so I thought he'd enjoy a day out at my expense. The next meeting was on the following Tuesday so we fixed it for Terry to go up and meet him there. What happened next I do not know. Whether Terry got into conversation with the two who killed him and gave the impression that he was picking up something valuable, or whether they thought it was sure to be worth pinching as Terry was driving a BMW, I don't know, and Terry isn't here to tell us. But he got into a fight and they told Gary that they were to pick up the case. I wonder how he is? I haven't rung him lately.'

'He was worried because he thought he owed you ten thousand pounds.'

'Ha! Where would I get ten grand? And if I had it, would I trust a stranger to pick it up for me? No, that's a crazy idea. I'll definitely have to ring him to stop him worrying.'

'Well, I can save you the phone call, Gary Baker was killed last week.'

Vince was visibly shocked. He was momentarily lost for words. Then

'Who would have done it? He was a nice guy. I liked him.'

'I was hoping you could have some idea of who could have done it. What about the two who took your suitcase? Could it be them? Who are they?

'No idea. Honestly. I'm sorry. Can't help.'

Dave decided to finish here and made to depart.

'I'll go then. Thanks for talking to me. By the way, do you know where Megan has gone to?

Vince looked surprised.

'No. I've no idea of that either.'

Dave left a very sad and puzzled man in that room. He had mentioned Megan purely to sow the seeds of doubt in Spivey's mind. He would be thinking that if the police knew about Megan, what else did they know? Have they interviewed Megan? If so, would her story tally with his? If not, they would know he was lying. Vince's mind was churning with ideas. Which was what Dave wanted. Perhaps the next visit from the police would be more fruitful.

THIRTY FIVE

DI Diane Coleman picked up the phone.

'Hello. DI Coleman,' she announced.

'Hi Diane. It's Dave.'

'Nice to hear from you so soon.'

'Well, I thought I'd start the ball rolling. I've visited Mr Spivey. Just played it cool. Checking up that he'd got his car back OK and so on. He gave me a cock and bull story about getting Doctor Baker to collect some old clothes from his girlfriend, but Nick had already given us chapter and verse about that, so I didn't contradict him.'

'That's good. He'll be confidently thinking he's got us fooled. Anything else?'

'Yes. A few things. One – he seemed genuinely surprised to hear that Doctor Baker is dead but I didn't let on how he died. I'm sure his surprise wasn't an act, so you can let Nick know to bring his list up to date. Secondly, when I mentioned the ten grand he said it was being picked up, despite having said that the case only contained a few clothes. And finally - I asked if he knew where Megan has gone to. We hadn't mentioned her earlier, so he's not sure how much we know. He'll be very wary from now on, but he'll also be careful about his lies.'

'Thanks for that, Dave. I've got a couple of DC's in unmarked cars keeping tabs on his taxis. They seem to be visiting some of the run-down estates quite regularly but they're not doing supermarket runs and they're not carrying passengers. We'll be making a visit on him soon. An early morning visit, I think.'

'Good luck with that. I'll be on my way, now. If there's

anything else you need, you know where I am. I'll email my report to you when I get back'

They said their goodbyes and closed the call.

Diane blessed the day she had brought the coffee machine into the office. The standard of the drinks far exceeded the rubbish she had been offered when some of the staff made one for her. Having access to a latté at work was a luxury not available to many police stations. She put her cup down and tapped her keyboard to bring up the file on Vince Spivey. It was remarkably empty apart from a speeding ticket five years ago. She would add Dave's email when it arrived, probably that afternoon, when he had returned to his office in Colwyn Bay. She was musing over her next move when the phone rang.

'Hello. DI Coleman' she said.

'Hello, ma'am. PC Sandra Harper. Just reporting that I've seen a car with a skull and cross bones in the back window. I'm down near the Pier Head and it passed me a few minutes ago. It stopped at the lights so I've got a number for you. There were two men inside but I didn't get a proper look at them before it moved off. The car is a blue BMW.'

'That's excellent news, Sandra. We'll be on it right away. Thanks.'

'I'll give you a written report when I come in.'

Diane called across the office to DC Paddy Melia.

'Paddy, job for you. Run this number past DVLA, please. You and I might be making a visit shortly

Patrick Joseph Melia had the black hair and bright blue eyes common to so many of his countrymen. He was born in Limerick and his parents moved to Liverpool when he was a child. He had an Irish lilt to his speech and a winning smile which had an effect on Diane on those occasions when she had to remind herself that she was his boss, ten years his senior and not to be so bloody silly and anyway he's married.

Within ten minutes, Paddy had come across to her desk with the information she wanted.

'Blue BMW. Registered to Michael John Laggan. Lives out at Hale. According to our information, he runs a haulage business – Laggan Logistics, from a private yard at Wavertree. Good spot for a haulage firm, convenient for the M62. He's got 23 employees. Mechanics and drivers plus a couple of office staff,' was his report.

'Thanks for that, Paddy.' She filled him in on the Bangor Races murder and said they would need to visit the yard and check out the car. She also rang Dave Tudor. He was still on his way home and was quite agreeable for Diane to make preliminary enquiries in his case. A final call to Nick Price to bring him up to date on what was happening as a result of Dave's visit to Vince Spivey and she was ready to leave.

It was a short journey to Wavertree and they drove into the yard and parked in front of the office building. As they got out of the car, they made a swift appraisal of the various vehicles parked on the yard. An artic was pulling out of the warehouse and heading for the gate. A white van was parked in front of the garage opposite the offices and a variety of private cars were parked in a small park between the garage and the road – presumably staff cars. Among them was a blue BMW. Diane had memorised the registration number and checked the number plate. It was the same. And in the rear window was a skull and cross bones sticker. She led the way into the reception area where a receptionist was about to welcome them to Laggan Logistics when the door behind her opened and Mick Laggan emerged from his office to take over proceedings.

'What can I do for the law today? One of my lads been speeding?' he was trying to be jovial but it didn't wash with Diane. Excess joviality usually represented an attempt to cover up guilt, in her experience. A false air of nothing to worry about.

'Shall we go into your office. I take it you are Mr Laggan.'

'Yes, come this way. Sorry, I should have introduced myself. Mick Laggan.

'And I'm DI Coleman. This is DC Melia.' She showed her warrant card.

They followed him into the office and he closed the door. It was a small office with not a scrap of paper in sight. A monitor showed where lorries were, with little dots moving along motorways on a map of the UK. A pile of box files stood on the end of the desk. The top one was marked 'CORRESPONDENCE' so Diane assumed that this was the repository for the paperwork that she expected to see on the desk.

'What a neat office,' she remarked, 'I must say I was expecting something quite different.'

'I like to keep things away from prying eyes. Paperwork lying on the desk can be read by anyone. The staff, including the drivers and mechanics, come in here from time to time and they're experts at making a mountain out of a molehill after a glance at letters or invoices. So that's

211

my system; safe and simple.'

'Very commendable,' Diane commented.

Mick was anxious to know the reason for the visit.

'Thanks for the compliment. Now I'm sure you didn't come here to check my tidiness, so what brings you here today?'

'We're interested in your car, the BMW parked outside. Can you tell me where it has been in the last few weeks?'

'That's an interesting question,' Mick said, his hand moving across the desk towards the mouse which lay on the right-hand side.

Diane was quick to respond.

'I'd prefer it if you didn't touch the mouse, or any of the power switches. If you do, I shall have to arrest you on the spot.'

'What for? Handling a mouse?' He laughed, but nervously.

'As an accessory to murder, perverting the course of justice, take your pick.' She was not joking. 'Thank you.' she said as his hand was immediately retracted. 'I see you have a tracking system for all your vehicles. Is there a tracker on your BMW?'

'Yes, but I haven't been anywhere outside Liverpool for ages.'

'It's not you we're asking about. Just your car. Does anyone else drive it?'

'The lads on the yard sometimes. Running errands for me occasionally.'

'Right. I would like all the recordings of your trackers for the last month, please, together with a list of your staff. Do you have these on disc?' Mick nodded, reached into a drawer and passed over a bundle of discs. 'I'd also like the keys of the BMW so that I can take it away for examination. I'll take those now, if you don't mind.' She held out her hand as he passed the keys over from the key rack on the wall and she dropped them into a plastic evidence bag.

'I still don't understand,' he said. 'You mentioned murder and you want to take my car.'

'A man was murdered at Bangor Racecourse. Your car was there.'

'So were hundreds of other cars I should think.'

'But they weren't picking up a suitcase. Yours was. Our evidence connects these events. We'll be in touch. Thank you for your co-operation.' Diane stood up and she and Paddy left.

Once outside, she checked that the BMW was locked and rang the station. She arranged for the BMW to be collected on a low loader and a team organised to examine the discs. She needed quick results and Diane Coleman was not good at waiting for results. On the way they saw the low loader in the opposite lane, on its way to the pick-up and she arrived back to find the digital team eagerly awaiting the discs like slavering dogs waiting impatiently for their supper. This was the part of the job she enjoyed. Over a cup of coffee from her machine, she rang Dave Tudor and brought him up to speed on what she had done. It was his case, after all, but she needed to secure the evidence before anyone had chance to hide it. Dave was grateful. He would be back tomorrow.

The next morning, the digital team were in a position to

draw conclusions about the tracker discs. Detective Sergeant Jimmy Catherall was the computer king in the digital team and he took on the task of explaining their findings to Diane.

'Keep it simple for me, Jimmy,' she had instructed.

'Don't worry, if Mick Laggan can understand this, you'll have no trouble with it, and you can be sure he understood it perfectly. It's a brilliant tracking system designed for busy bosses.'

Diane filled her coffee cup again and settled down to pay attention.

'To start with, we have a map showing all the vehicle journeys day by day and you can use the calendar to check whichever day you are interested in. Now most of Laggan's business is between the East Coast and the North West, from Felixstowe, Lowestoft and Harwich to Warrington and further North. This program shows the lorry number alongside each track, and you can see that the bulk of the journeys are on the east to west route I mentioned.'

Diane pointed to two tracks which did not follow the others. 'What's happening there? Diversion for road works, accidents?' she asked.

'Those were our first ideas,' Jimmy went on, 'but when we checked there were no diversions on that day, not in that area anyway.'

'So what's happening?'

'Well, if they went that far off course, as you might say, there must have been a good reason and for two of them to do it on different days it must have been a very good reason. The track goes out as far as Hereford and Worcester. What comes to mind if I mention those two

214

counties?'

'Fruit. Cider. Hops'

'Exactly. And fruit picking needs workers. Cheap workers.'

'You're not suggesting immigrant workers?' Diane was warming to the thrill of the chase. 'Do we know exactly where they went?'

'We've checked their tachographs and we can pin down the exact farms they went to. So far we haven't found any invoices for that part of the world, which there would be if they were on legitimate business there, so it seems that Mr Laggan does carry more than goods around the country.'

"Has anyone been in touch with the West Mercia force yet?' Diane wanted to know.

'No, we left that for you.' Jimmy smiled as he passed the job on to Diane.

'Fair enough,' she said and reached for the phone, 'And let me have a written brief in ...' she looked at the clock...'an hour' The smile left Jimmy's face as quickly as it had arrived as he set about committing his findings to paper.

THIRTY SIX

'Doctor Maitland is here for you,' Helen said into the phone and nodded at the reply. She put her phone down.

'Mr Upton is free now,' she reported and David Maitland passed through into Mr Upton's office.

'Strange you should ask to see me this morning,' Michael Upton began, 'because I wanted to put something to you. I won't keep you, but I've had a notification of a conference you might still be interested in. You may remember we applied for tickets previously, but as places were limited, we were balloted out. They now find that, as a result of cancellations, there are places available. I'm wondering if you would care to attend at fairly short notice. It takes place in Manchester in two weeks' time.'

He slid a sheet of paper across the desk. 'These are the details.'

David picked it up and read,' World Conference on Cardiology and Cardiovascular Medicine. It sounds just up my street, I must say I was disappointed to be balloted out last time. Manchester isn't very far away either. The last one of these was held in Miami. That was five years ago.'

'I'm glad you're keen to go. Apparently, it will bring together world class Cardiologists of all sorts including nursing staff to discuss strategies and advancements in Cardiology.'

'Thanks for letting me know. We've got a busy time ahead at home. My mother-in-law is unwell – she's been seeing Jim Parton….'

'Oh, cancer,' Upton interrupted.

'Yes, it's devastating news, but she has kept her condition secret from the family for some time. Didn't want to upset us. She's always been very independent. Now the cancer is spreading and she finally informed us last night that she is close to the end. Sadly, there's nothing more Jim can do for her.'

'That is sad news,' Michael Upton put in. 'How is Chrissy taking it? She must be at her wits' end. Amazing woman, Alex. To keep her condition secret like that.'

'Yes. I've had a word with Jim this morning. He said she was adamant that we shouldn't know about her visits here and, of course, he couldn't say anything to me, patient confidentiality and all that. Chrissy and the kids are distraught, as you might guess. I'll need some time off to be with them. Which is what I wanted to see you about.'

'Of course. We'll arrange for a locum to cover for you. Take all the time you need.'

David nodded his head in thanks and returned to his office to update his secretary about the new situation, then set off for home.

At home, he found Chrissy in tears, as he had left her. Alex had been her rock throughout her life and had shown no outward signs of ill-health. She had maintained an active life right to the end, her planning for the future – including the new dress for the Summer Ball, passing off her occasional weaknesses as old age and dieting, Chrissy had been taken in by it all and the sudden announcement of her mother's imminent demise had come as a real shock. Maddy had kept her supplied with tea but the tears kept coming; it would be a long time before they stopped for even a temporary break.

Once again, bereavement was going to affect Maddy's young life, first her grandfather, then Gary, now she was about to lose her beloved Gran. Her world was turning upside down. The girl was mystified by it all. Her mother was tearful, yet her Gran was stoic, even planning her own funeral; Maddy could not comprehend the difference in the two reactions. She could not picture a life without her Gran being at the bungalow. There would be strangers living there; that would be difficult, to say the least.

David was used to dealing with problems of life and death at work, but when they become personal, professional training doesn't help. The effect on Chrissy of losing Alex would be almost insurmountable. The common phrase of 'Time is a great healer' is no comfort at times like this; it comes much later. He would have his work cut out to nurse his wife through the next few weeks. He could not imagine why Alex had kept her cancer secret from the family. Something to do with her image of the little toughie, perhaps. Or was it a misguided attempt to save the family from worry? He realised that he would miss her as much as everyone else. She had helped him through some rocky times early in his marriage and more recently when his father had died. Had she known then about her own condition? he asked himself. Little Toughie again. And now he knew that he had to be strong for Chrissy and the kids.

Jon was devastated. Like Maddy, he found bereavement a harrowing new experience when his grandfather died; impending bereavement was even worse, like waiting for the axe to fall. He loved his Gran and she made no secret of the fact that Jon was her favourite, though she was careful to treat both grandchildren alike. She had always admired strong character in a man and she was proud of the way Jon was growing into the kind of man with whom she had surrounded herself all her working life. Jon was going to miss her guidance, her generosity and her love.

THIRTY SEVEN

Diane shielded her eyes against the low, early-morning sun. Five o'clock was an early start for her; normally she slept till seven, but adrenalin had her awake by four, showered, fed and dressed by four thirty and marshalling her troops by five.

Dave Tudor had had an early start from North Wales. Having seen Jimmy's report, he was to bring in Mick Laggan as a suspect in the Bangor murder. Diane would see to the immigrant workers case later following a few more phone calls and farm visits.

PC Bill Fryer, built like a brick outhouse, could probably have dealt with a locked door with his bare hands, but with his trusty ram, which he had nicknamed Thumper, in his grip the job would be done more explosively and with more noise, both features designed to create more confusion among the residents, who would no doubt be rushing round trying to hide anything that could be used as evidence against them.

With the door demolished, first in would be PC Stuart Ruskin. His ability to take in situations quickly was essential for an armed officer. Diane hoped that his weapon would be redundant today, that the noise and confusion caused by the other officers flooding into his house would be sufficient to stun Vince Spivey into immediate submission,

Bill and Thumper had done their work well, the troops were even now searching the house and Vince was sitting in an interview room rehearsing his lies, while Diane was studying the report from the digital team about Mick

Laggan's tracking system.

'Let's have a word with Mr Spivey,' she said at last, and she and Patrick Melia gathered the paperwork and made their way to the interview room. After the formalities, she sat and faced Vince Spivey, who seemed relaxed as Diane opened the file and took out some papers.

'I don't want to be messing about with these 'no comment' answers so we'll cut to the chase,' she said. 'A large quantity of drugs was found at your house this morning. Would you care to tell us where it came from?'

Vince shrugged. 'Father Christmas must have left them.' He had a twisted grin on his face, pleased with his own cleverness.

'Oh. That makes it easy,' Diane said. 'We won't be able to interview him until December, so you'll have all that time in a cell until we can confirm your story.' She started to gather up the papers, preparing to leave.

'Hang on a minute!' The prospect of four months in a cell had an electric effect on Vince, 'I was only joking. You must realise that.'

She resumed her seat. 'I don't have time for jokes, especially in a serious matter like this. Let's try another question. A friend of yours was at Bangor races in your car. Would you care to explain?'

Vince repeated the story as given to Dave Tudor, including the case of old clothes, the presumed fight and the loss of his friend, Terry. When he mentioned Gary as his courier, he went on to say that he understood that Gary was dead. 'I liked the feller. It wasn't me who knifed him.'

'Knifed him? Why do you say that?'

'I just assumed. Knifing seems to be the way, these days,

221

and if it was the same ones that did for Terry, then they used the knife again.'

Diane made a note, but didn't divulge how Gary had died. 'That's very interesting. Any idea who they might be?'

'No. sorry'

'I'm sure you do know who they are but you want to take revenge yourself. That will be a long time coming, because the amount of drugs we found in your house will see you going away for quite a few years. So, would you like to think again?'

'No.'

'Not if I can put in a word for you? It might reduce your sentence in the long run. Surely that would be worthwhile?'

'I'll take my chances.'

'OK. Please yourself. Why did Gary Baker think he owed you ten thousand pounds?'

'Because he did.'

'It was in the suitcase, wasn't it? Amongst the clothes you put in as camouflage. And whoever killed Terry took the case. Am I right?'

'You seem to think so.'

'At least two witnesses say I am, but it would help if you would confirm it for me.'

And so the tennis match went on, with Diane asking probing questions and Vince playing defensive drop shots which kept the game going without adding anything to the spectacle.

A constable came in and handed Diane a note which she read and asked the constable to 'Tell him to put him in Room 3.' Mick Laggan was now helping the police with their enquiries, enquiries that would continue in Room 3 when she had finished with Vince Spivey.

'That will be all for now,' she said to Vince and asked the constable to return him to the cells. As they walked into the corridor Diane, who was bringing up the rear, heard loud voices and the beginnings of a scuffle. In the few seconds which it took for her to reach the door and look out into the corridor, one constable was sprawled on the floor, his nose streaming with blood, another was trying to separate Laggan and Spivey, who were swapping blows, the desk sergeant was opening the door at the end of the corridor, wondering what the noise was all about.

'So it's you that's grassed me up,' Mick Laggan was obviously the aggrieved party. 'Told 'em everything, have you?'

'I've said nothing about you or Slug and Slime!' Vince was on the defensive as Mick swung another blow at his head.

The desk sergeant had retreated back to his desk but signalled to Bill Fryer, who was conveniently in the office. Bill relished a bit of action and rushed into the corridor, grabbed Mick by the lapels and flung him into Interview Room 3 in one smooth action. He looked round. 'Who's next?'

Vince put up both hands. 'Not me. I'm on my way to the cells.'

Bill looked to Diane for confirmation, she nodded, and the constable escorted Vince peacefully to his cell, Mick's threats echoing down the corridor behind him.

Diane made her way to her office. 'We'll give him time to cool off, then I have a few questions for Mr Laggan.

Perhaps assaulting a policeman might be added to the list of charges.'

Dave Tudor was sitting in her office when she arrived. 'I just had a word with the desk sergeant,' he explained, 'Did I hear some fisticuffs going on as I came in?'

'Yes. You've brought Mick Laggan in, thanks, and he thinks Vince Spivey has grassed him up. Unfortunately, they met in the corridor, with the inevitable result.'

'And did Vince really grass him up?' Dave asked.

'No way. He's kept very quiet about this. There's more to their relationship than we think. I wonder how far back it goes. What does Mick think Vince has told us? Was he talking about the murder or the people trafficking? We'll have to find out. Paddy!' she called across the office. Can you do a check on Laggan and Spivey. See if their paths have crossed before. I think there's a bit of aggro in their history.'

'Right, boss. I'm on it.'

She turned to Dave. 'We seem to have the main suspects in all these cases, so perhaps it's time to get Nick up here to iron out the details. Both of these were on his list for the hit-and-run. Let's see if he can come up this afternoon.'

She picked up the phone and dialled Nick's number. He answered swiftly and agreed to go up to Liverpool. The prospect of tackling a couple of suspects was highly attractive.

The afternoon started off busily for Diane. Jimmy Catherall came down with a report on the tracker discs. 'We've also looked at the records for the two vehicles which went to Herefordshire. Here are the names of the drivers –

224

no criminal records – the addresses of the farms they went to and a list of all other journeys they've done, some in other vehicles of Laggan's.'

'This is good stuff. Thanks, Jimmy.'

'I've spoken to DI Mervyn Allsop at West Mercia about the Hereford farms and I said you would be in touch as soon as poss. He's keen to get down to Hereford, but he'll wait for your say-so. He didn't want to do anything that might influence your case. All the phone numbers you'll need are on this sheet.' Yet another page was passed over.

'You seem to have thought of everything, Jimmy. Well done.'

'All part of the service' he grinned, as he closed the door behind him.

'A good lad, that, he'll be ….' Dave was saying as a knock on the door preceded the entry of a constable from the forensic team.

'DC Wells, Forensics,' he introduced himself. 'We've been examining the BMW and here's a preliminary report. We've found a blood-stain – on the sun visor. They always forget to wipe those off. We're checking it against the murder victim's blood group – we'll report later. There are also two or three sets of prints that we haven't identified yet. Perhaps your investigations will throw up a few candidates.'

Diane thanked him and he left.

'This is a breakthrough for you, Dave,' Diane said, passing the report over to him.

Her next task was to ring Mervyn Allsop at West Mercia. He sounded keen to get to grips with the case and she filled him in on all the relevant information. She suggested that he got down to Hereford as soon as possible and she would leave it to him to decide if and when Border Force should be contacted, based on what he found.

She was back at the coffee machine when the door opened again. Paddy Melia brought in more paper.

'I thought this was supposed to be a paperless society,' Diane said, though her imagination really preferred Paddy bringing in paper to reading an email.

'The history of Laggan and Spivey, chapter and verse,' Paddy announced. 'Both the same age. Both went to Perton Road Junior School. Lots of rivalry, no doubt because one was blue and one was red. (That's important in Liverpool). I've visited Laggan's yard and chatted around. It seems that most drivers do the bread-and-butter driving, from the ports to the warehouses, but there are two who do the odd ones – different destinations and special cargoes. I turned the Irish charm on one of the secretaries …'

'Lucky girl,' thought Diane.

'…and she mentioned Eddie and Robbie. She called them Slug and Slime.' A bell rang in Diane's head. He went on,' It's their nickname around the yard. Not very complimentary, is it? She also mentioned a girl called Megan, Laggan's niece, who used to work for Spivey. She said there was some history there but she didn't know the full story.'

Diane flicked through Jimmy's report. 'Here we are. Edward Norman and Robert West. On the list as driving other vehicles. Vince mentioned Slug and Slime when they were arguing in the corridor. Paddy, take Pete Walton and Bill Fryer over to the yard and bring those two in. Suspected of murder of Terry Burton. Off you go!'

A tap at the door announced the arrival of Nick Price.

'Good to see you again, Nick,' Dave Tudor said. 'It's all happening here at the moment.'

'Hi, Nick!' Diane waved from her desk. 'Can you fill Nick in, please, Dave?'

'Of course. Glad to. I've been an observer for too long,' he said, and proceeded to take Nick through the day's events. By the time he had finished, Eddie and Robbie were safely in the cells and the three DI's were ready to start their investigations.

All the reports had been copied so that Dave and Nick had their own copies and a list had been drawn up which showed that Vince Spivey was under suspicion for drug dealing and Gary's murder, Mick Laggan, for people trafficking and Gary's murder with an additional charge of assaulting a police officer now added on. Eddie and Robbie were held for Terry's murder.

'Nick and I will start in Room 3. Mick will have cooled off a bit by now, Diane said as she prepared to leave the office. 'Dave, Eddie and Robbie are yours. Nice and straightforward. Use rooms 1 and 2.'

Mick sat in Room 3 with a constable watching over him. He drummed his fingers on the table in a false display of boredom. Internally, he was far from bored. His mind was buzzing. Had the cops worked out anything from the tracker discs? Let's hope they don't pull in Eddie and Robbie; if they do we'll be in real trouble. There's that kid they kidnapped the other night. Nobody's mentioned him. Good job they took him back. I had nothing to do with killing Terry. We were kind of mates in the old days. Would

I have done that to him? It must be Vince who grassed me up. Tit for tat for me swiping his ten grand. So what have they got him in for? His train of thought came to an abrupt halt when the door opened and Diane and Nick entered the room.

'Your solicitor has just arrived, he'll be in in a moment,' she announced, 'Ah, here he is. I'll give you five minutes together then we'll come back.

Gerrard Potter thanked her, shook hands with Mick, who now looked more relieved, and sat down at the table. They chatted for the full five minutes until Diane and Nick returned and sat opposite.

She told the tape machine the date and time and who was present'

Mr Potter said, 'You said DI Price from Cheshire Constabulary. That's unusual. Why is he here?'

'Fair question,' Diane said. 'Crime knows no boundaries, as you know, but we find it helps if investigating officers from the relevant areas can co-operate. It saves your client, for instance, being interviewed twice in different places. I hope you see that as acceptable.' Potter nodded.

Diane pushed two sheets of paper across the table. 'This is a print out from your tracker discs showing a week's journeys for your lorries, and this is a print out of just two of those vehicles also shown on the first sheet. The bulk of the journeys are from the East coast to the North West, but these two take a different route home. Can you explain why?'

'Not really,' Mick felt confident. 'They were experienced drivers, so if they make a detour, it's for a good reason. I don't question them when they get back. They would tell me if it was anything serious. It was probably a road closed for road works or a crash, it happens all the time.'

'But only for these two drivers, it seems.'

'How do you mean, Inspector?' Potter interjected.

Diane selected three other sheets from her pile, identified by pink tabs.

'Because these sheets from dates a month apart show the same lorries making the same detour.'

Mick woke up. 'They would have had business in that area. Not all our drops are in the north west.' 'Get out of that,' he thought.

'I'm afraid that any business you had in that area was illegal. Your records show no invoices, there are no payments into your bank from firms in that area. And our colleagues from West Mercia Police are in attendance at Knott's Dyke Farm...' Mick flinched. '...as we speak.'

'I don't see what you're driving at, Inspector,' Potter said. 'There's nothing to stop a lorry driver taking an extra load if he's empty on the way back.'

'There is if that load is human and foreign and illegal.'

The penny dropped. Potter looked at Mick, who had visibly sagged with a helpless look on his face.

Mick knew when he was beaten. 'You'll have to prove it,' he snarled.

Potter spoke up. 'I think I need more time with my client, in the light of this.'

'Very well,' Diane said. 'We'll give you ten minutes later. For now, DI Price has some questions on another matter.'

'You still haven't explained the presence of a DI from Cheshire.'

Nick replied. 'I'm here for a different investigation, with

which your client may be able to help. I'd appreciate it if he could be equally frank with me as he has been with DI Coleman.'

'What do you want to know? I've done nothing in Cheshire, I'm sure.' Mick was dejected but defiant. Cheshire was firmer ground.

'It's to do with a doctor called Gary Baker.' Nick began.

'Doesn't ring a bell.'

'What if I say Megan; ten grand; Bangor Races. Any bells ringing yet?'

'Yes, but the Baker one still doesn't mean anything.'

'He took the money from Megan to Bangor Races, where I understand your men picked it up.'

'Ri-ight' Where is this going? Mick wondered.

'Were you at Bangor that day?'

'No, and I can prove it.'

'No need. I believe you.' Nick needed to gain Mick's confidence and he knew that there were only two receding figures on the Bangor CCTV.

'It's just that Doctor Baker was killed recently…'

'What? And you thought that I'd done it? It's not my style. Why would I kill him?'

'To stop him telling the police all he knew about the killing at Bangor perhaps?'

'Well you can stop perhapsing. How was he killed? Shot? I haven't got a gun. Knifed? I haven't got a knife. Pushed under a bus? I haven't been to Cheshire in ages. Sorry, you need to look somewhere else.'

'I'm inclined to believe you. But you do have a motive, so I'm keeping an open mind for now. Thank you. Interview terminated at fifteen-ten.

At fifteen-fifteen Diane and Nick walked into Room 4, where Vince Spivey sat. His drugs case was open and shut. The supplies had been found in his house, his taxi drivers had been questioned and remanded where necessary, enough evidence had been gathered to put him away for a very long time. Diane introduced Nick into the conversation, explaining that he was involved in a murder investigation.

'If it's about Terry, you're talking to the wrong man,' he said, unprompted.

'No, it's about Doctor Baker. You knew him, I believe.'

'Yes. I've already spoken to the other man from Wales about him.'

'Yes, he told me. And you know that Doctor Baker is dead?'

'Yes. He was a nice man. Perhaps I shouldn't have got him involved, but the chance of some free morphine was too good to miss. If he'd have done a couple of trips for me, I'd have let him off the hook. I'm not daft. I could see that we couldn't go on like that for ever. When I was mobile again that would have been it. The end,'

'And as it is, he's come to the end.'

'How did it finish, for him, I mean?'

'Let's just. say it was a road accident. Except it might not have been an accident.'

'So you think I might have crashed his car? Why would I? If it was to keep him quiet, I'd have to see off the lad, his driver, too, and Megan, wherever she is. Do I look like a mass killer? Sorry. Wrong man.'

Nick was finished. 'OK, Vince.'

Diane lifted a finger, 'Just one more question. Yesterday

you told me I should ask those who did for Terry. Those. Plural. And in the scuffle with Mick Laggan you mentioned Slug and Slime. Were you thinking that they had anything to do with the death of Doctor Baker?'

'I'm not a grass, Ms Coleman and you're not daft. You know I can't answer that and I know you will come to the right conclusion.' A knowing look passed between them.

Nick felt that he was spoiling the moment when he asked, 'By the way, Why Slug and Slime?'

Vince said, 'Where one goes the other is sure to follow. They're inseparable. Robbie's useless on his own.'

Dave Tudor had had the pleasure of the company of Eddie and Robbie all afternoon and it had not taken much to confirm that it was they who had fought with Terry and even that it was Robbie who had actually delivered the fatal stabbing. Where Eddie had denied everything with a 'Prove it' attitude, Robbie had been easy to break down.

Dave had been relaxed, talked about the day out at the races. 'It's great there in the summer, but when the sun's over the mountains it makes driving difficult when you're leaving.' Robbie had agreed wholeheartedly 'I even had to put the sun visor thing down as we left.'

Game, set and match.

Nick had had a word with Eddie at the end of Dave's interview. As Eddie was a little truculent, he took a softly, softly approach, engaging in conversation rather than questioning.

Had they enjoyed their day's racing? Were they into any other sports? He was a Stockport County supporter

232

himself, what about you? Liverpool? Everton? Eddie preferred Tranmere Rovers.

Nick reached down and laid a transparent evidence bag on the table, revealing a blue and white scarf within. Eddie let out an involuntary 'Ah!' in recognition.

'You recognise it, then?' Nick said.

Eddie nodded, sheepishly, wishing he had kept quiet.

The trap was sprung.

Jon's captors were revealed. Nick confirmed this later from the tracker discs. The white van had been in Thornhill on consecutive nights last week.

He could add kidnapping to the list of charges.

THIRTY EIGHT

'Penny for them.'

'What? Oh, sorry. Deep in thought.'

'It's this case, isn't it?'

Nick and Helen sat on a bench facing the river. Sunday together in Chester had been enjoyable. Morning coffee at the Grosvenor and a walk around the Rows were followed by a light lunch at a little restaurant in the shadow of the cathedral. In the afternoon, Nick had been a spectator at a hectic, very rough and seemingly dangerous wheelchair basketball match in which Helen took part. An evening meal at a pub overlooking the river rounded off a perfect day. As Nick relaxed, the case was never very far from his mind.

Taking equal space in his mind was the basketball match in the afternoon. Helen was a tigress. Where Nick was flinching at the sight and sound of two chairs colliding, Helen seemed to relish the hurly-burly of the game. No quarter was given or asked; she was the equal of her male team-mates and she emerged unscathed as the full-time whistle was blown by the referee.

'Yes,' he replied, 'the case and your match this afternoon. You were brilliant. I was very impressed. The speed of the game and the way you all spun the chairs to change direction were amazing.'

'I'm glad you enjoyed it. You must come with me again.'

'I'll be glad to.'

'So, what about the case?

'I'm still no nearer to finding out who killed Gary Baker. I suppose I was guilty of expecting the people in Liverpool to be the guilty parties as they were already involved in crime and might have killed him to keep him quiet, but one by one we found that they couldn't have done it, so I'm thrown back on the people at Thornhill – unless it was an accident or by someone so far unknown to us.'

'Had Doctor Baker upset anyone else that you know of?' she asked.

'No. I suppose you don't know, from the inside, whether any patients or staff had a grudge?'

'Nothing has been reported to us in the office and we see all the complaints. What if it was an accident, a drunk driver on his way home perhaps.'

'Sorry, no. It was Gary's own car and we saw the driver on the CCTV from Green Shoots Garden Centre. He wasn't drunk. So, tomorrow morning's job will be to go through my list of suspects again. Let's forget it for tonight and enjoy the rest of our evening.

'That's an awfully good idea,' Helen murmured, sliding closer to him on the bench.' Nick ordered fresh drinks from a passing waiter, slipped his arm around Helen's shoulders and they shared a kiss.'

'A day to remember.' he sighed.

THIRTY NINE

Nick sat at his desk next morning and drew up a list of his suspects once more. A fresh look may bring on a Eureka moment.

Top of the list was David Maitland. Was his distrust of Gary sufficient for him to commit murder? He had been stung by the theft of the pills which Gary had pinned on him, but that had been cleared up. You never knew what prompted people to commit crimes, but David wasn't under pressure at work and, really, he wasn't the type – whatever that was. He still scored six or seven

Chrissy was next. Now here was a reason. Eighteen years of worry and deceit. Nothing had happened to change his mind about her score of four, so there it stayed,

Jon Maitland was thought to have run away, which warranted a score of 9, but now the tracker sheets had shown the white van's visits to Thornhill, it was clear that Jon was telling the truth so he went down to six.

Maddy and Barry Meadows would still be at one and two and the two high scorers, Vince and the BMW boys had proved themselves innocent of the hit-and-run, so were off the list.

An interview with the family would be necessary. He would need all his tact to talk them into even considering an interview. He should bear in mind that they all had access to the key of Gary's car.

Maddy answered the phone when he rang.

'Hello, Maddy. It's DI Price. Are either your Mum or Dad available, please?'

'Sorry,' she said. 'Dad's preparing for a conference in

Manchester and doesn't want to be disturbed and Mum's down at the hospital.'

'Oh, dear. Is she alright?'

'Yes, she's fine, but they've taken my Gran in, She's very ill.'

He heard her voice trembling as she said it; obviously it was serious. This could wait.

'Alright, I'll leave it until tomorrow. Thank you. Bye.'

He spent the afternoon tidying up the loose ends on the other cases and writing up his reports. He read and re-read the forensic reports but there was nothing suspicious about the car. Had he missed a suspect? What about Sheryl? No, she was with Gary when it happened. Who was Megan who was mentioned? Someone would have hinted or some clue would have pointed to her. He finally gave up, rang Helen to say he would pick her up after work and they could go to the Cumberland Arms for a meal and a drink, to which she readily agreed.

An hour later, he was pushing Helen's chair along the corridor towards the exit when he met Jon leaving Ward 10.

'Hi, Jon. How's your Gran?' he asked.

'She's not very well at all,' Jon replied.

A distraught Chrissy appeared at the ward entrance.

'Jon, will you get...Oh, hello Inspector Price, I didn't expect to see you here.'

'Just picking up Helen to go out for the evening.'

He introduced them. He had told Helen about Alex and she sympathised with Chrissy.

'I was sorry to hear about your mother. How is she?'

'Mum's very poorly, I'm afraid. She's kept it secret until the last minute to save us the worry. She's so brave. Still

237

interested in everything. She was a news reporter, you know. You may remember, Zandra Martin. On television. She was asking how your investigation was going. I said 'Mum, I can't ask him that. You're not a reporter any more.'

'I'd be glad to tell her, if that will help her to rest. Her experience might help me to solve it. I'll be brief, though. I won't tire her out. Ask her.'

'I know my Mum. She'd love it! To get an update before anyone else? Heaven. I'll tell her you're here.'

Alex lay in bed, surrounded by tubes and machines which bleeped and blinked in response to the rhythms of her failing body. She brightened slightly at the prospect of a scoop, as she called it as Nick and Helen were introduced.

Nick began by saying how frustrating it was to have whittled down his suspects and to have come to a dead end.

'Perhaps you haven't looked far enough,' Alex suggested.

'Obviously not, but I can't think of anywhere else to look.'

Alex cleared her throat as she tried to sit up. 'I hate lying down. It feels like I'm drowning in my own saliva,' she explained, then went on,

'What about the description of the driver? Doesn't that help?'

'Sheryl said she only got a glimpse. She said he had short grey hair. Could be anybody.'

More rattling breaths followed, then she said

'And what about fingerprints?'

'All accounted for.'

'Did the officer who took the car back make any comments about it?'

'I remember him saying it must have been driven by a midget. The seat was right forward and he had to move it right back to get in, Mind you, he's six feet four and had a job getting his legs in.'

Disappointment showed on Alex's face. Was it the unaccustomed inactivity of being bed-ridden?

'Well,' Alex said, 'You do seem short of evidence. I don't envy the police in cases like this.'

Chrissy interrupted. 'I think Mum's getting tired,'

'Perhaps we ought to be going?' Helen asked, taking the hint, to which Nick agreed. He manoeuvred her chair out into the corridor, having said, 'Goodnight and thank you for listening,' to Alex, who replied, 'Thank you, Inspector. I think you need to go over the facts again.'

They made their way out of the hospital.

Nick and Helen were very subdued at the Cumberland. Appetites had vanished, so they passed on a meal, making do with a snack with their drinks

'Alex seemed a little disappointed when we were leaving, as though she had hoped to solve your case for you,' Helen said.

'Yes. It's the reporter in her. They never lose that investigative attitude. She went straight to the heart of the matter. Straight questions. On the ball. Almost as though she knew where her questions were leading.'

He looked thoughtful, then hit his forehead with the heel of his hand.

'Of course. What an idiot. It's obvious. Come on, drink up.'

Helen drank up, then spun her chair round and asked, 'Where are we going?'

'Back to the hospital,' Nick said.

'It's late. Won't tomorrow do?'

'Tomorrow may be too late!'

A slightly puzzled Helen complied as Nick pushed at speed down the corridor of Aggies again. She was sure all would become clear eventually. Arriving at Ward 10, Nick paused for breath, then tapped the door.

Chrissy opened the door and was surprised to see Nick and Helen.

'Inspector!' she said.

'I'm sorry to intrude again, but may I see your Mum for a moment, please? It's really important.'

Chrissy could not see what could be important after Alex's previous brief conversation with Nick and was preparing to ask him nicely not to bother them, but a voice from the bed said, 'Is that the Inspector? Let him in, please, Chrissy.'

'Thank you,' Nick said as he pushed Helen's chair into the room.

'I knew you'd be back when you'd time to think,' Alex said.

'Yes. I went over your questions time and again. All the way through this investigation, we have assumed that we were looking for a man. Sheryl described the driver as 'He had grey hair' and nobody questioned it. But I think if we were to say 'She had grey hair, and was short, and had access to the key of the car, we might have got to the truth quicker.'

'At last,' Alex said, with a smile that was a mixture of relief and triumph; relief that she had made her confession, triumph that her plans had paid off and led the policeman to the truth.

Chrissy was dumbfounded. 'I don't understand! What are you saying? That my Mum...'

She couldn't bring herself to say it. She hugged her mother despite the festoon of tubes surrounding her.

'Why? Oh, why would you do such a thing?' The tears were flowing freely.

Alex took a deep breath and summoned her weakening body once more.

'You're right. I did it. When I heard that Gary had been collecting drug money and taking Jon with him, I couldn't contain myself. Not my Jonathan. I've seen too much of the drug scene in my life. All I have done in the past is report bad things, never a chance to put things right. The only way I could save Jon was to get rid of Gary. A short time ago, Gary came to see me, asking for a loan. He was in debt and imagined that I was well off enough to lend him ten thousand pounds. I said I would think about it and in our conversation, I laughingly suggested he find someone to blackmail. 'Everybody has a secret,' I joked. 'You might be lucky.' He must have been so desperate that he took me seriously. And when I got my diagnosis from Doctor Parton saying I only had weeks rather than months to live, I decided that this was my only chance to do something positive against the drug dealers. I knew where Jon kept the key for Gary's car – it was easy just to pick it up off the shelf – the rest you can work out for yourselves.'

The effort had taken so much energy, even Little Toughie was struggling. 'My time here is short; I hope I'll be forgiven.'

As Nick drove Helen home, their thoughts were all on

241

the case. 'Poor woman. To love her grandson that much. To drive her to commit murder,' said Helen, who had been moved to tears in the hospital. Nick was deep in thought. He would have to discuss this turn of events with Tom Cameron in the morning. It was inevitable that Alex would leave this world long before a case could be brought against her.

As well as visiting Alex at the hospital, Chrissy, Maddy and Jon spent the next day at home, consoling each other with the conflicting situations of Alex's illness and her confession. David was in Manchester at the international conference that Michael Upton had arranged for him.

The day had dragged interminably in the Maitland house until early evening, when David arrived home. As he opened the door he called out 'Chrissy, you'll never guess who I've brought to see you. Faces from the past!'

Chrissy hurriedly checked her make-up, ran her fingers through her hair and went to meet David's guests.

'It's Brett and Charlotte. Remember? Med school? Haven't seen them since. Off to Australia after our Stag and Hen do's.'

'Of course I remember. Are you at this conference?'

There were hugs and handshakes. Introductions to Jon and Maddy. They finally sat down to catch up on eighteen years news.

Charlotte was keen to tell a story. 'Last time I saw you, well, I don't know if I should tell the kids.' Then, in a mock conspiratorial, over-acted whisper for the kids' benefit, 'she was drunk.'

Jon smiled. 'It still happens from time to time.'

242

'Not like then,' Charlotte went on. 'We followed you along the road and you were with that creepy guy, what was his name?' She thought for a moment. 'Gary, that's right. At the bottom of that long staircase, you passed out so we took over. Brett carried you up to your room and I undressed you and put you to bed.'

'What happened to Gary?' Chrissy was glad that Jon had asked.

'He went off home. We wouldn't have let him into the nurses' home!'

The weight of eighteen years of worry dropped from Chrissy's shoulders. She looked across the room at Jon sitting next to his father.

She could say it now, with confidence.

His father.

ACKNOWLEDGEMENTS

My grateful thanks go to my wife, Rosemary, for her patient assistance in putting this story together.

Following my first book, Scarlet Feather, so many readers have enquired about my second that I am grateful to them all for their encouragement. They know who they are!

Printed in Great Britain
by Amazon